THE LAKE OF THE DEAD

Also available in Valancourt International

The Coming of Joachim Stiller
HUBERT LAMPO
Translated by Paul Vincent

A mild-mannered journalist's quiet life is suddenly upended by the intrusion of a mysterious figure called Joachim Stiller, who seems somehow to be controlling his life and destiny. It starts with an enigmatic letter – impossibly postmarked before he was even born – and as a series of strange phenomena ensues, he becomes obsessed with the question: Who is Joachim Stiller?

Intimations of Death
FELIX TIMMERMANS
Translated by Paul Vincent

Written after a near-death experience with a serious illness, this 1910 volume of macabre tales by a master of 20th-century Flemish literature is a collection of psychological horror stories worthy of Edgar Allan Poe.

The Tenant
ROLAND TOPOR
Translated by Francis K. Price

Desperate for a place to live, a Parisian moves into an apartment whose previous tenant hurled herself through the window, screaming. What happens next is a harrowing descent into paranoia and madness as a sequence of bizarre events unfolds that leaves the new tenant doubting his sanity and fearing for his life.

The Valancourt Book of World Horror Stories, vols. 1 & 2
EDITED BY JAMES D. JENKINS & RYAN CAGLE

These two volumes collect the best in contemporary horror from nearly forty countries around the world, translated from twenty-five different languages. The first volume was nominated for the World Fantasy Award and two Shirley Jackson Awards.

ANDRÉ BJERKE

Translated from the Norwegian by
James D. Jenkins

VALANCOURT BOOKS
Richmond, Virginia
MMXXII

The Lake of the Dead by André Bjerke
Originally published in Norwegian as *De dødes tjern* by H. Aschehoug
& Co. (W. Nygaard) AS, 1942
First Valancourt Books edition February 2022

Copyright © 1942 by André Bjerke
Translation, introduction, and notes © 2022 by James D. Jenkins

Published by Valancourt Books, Richmond, Virginia
http://www.valancourtbooks.com

ISBN 978-1-954321-11-3 (limited hardcover)
ISBN 978-1-954321-12-0 (trade paperback)

Cover by Ilan Sheady
Set in Dante MT

INTRODUCTION

[Rest assured: the following introduction is careful not to spoil the book for first-time readers. Although the novel is discussed in general terms, no important plot details are revealed beyond what is already disclosed on the back cover.]

IN 2001, A NORWEGIAN NEWSPAPER conducted a poll to determine the all-time best Norwegian crime novel. The winner was André Bjerke's *The Lake of the Dead* (1942), which beat the second-place finisher, a 1996 thriller by Karin Fossum, by over twenty percentage points. In a couple of similar polls conducted in more recent years, Bjerke has been knocked from the top spot by newer bestsellers by international superstars Fossum and Jo Nesbø, but even after all these years *The Lake of the Dead* never places lower than third. Given the book's enduring popularity in its own country (where it has also been filmed twice) and considering the appetite of American and British audiences for Nordic Noir over the past twenty-five years or so, it's surprising that no enterprising publisher has dusted off Bjerke's classic to make it available to a wider audience before now.

'But wait,' some readers are no doubt already saying, 'what's this about *crime novels*? Surely with a title like *The Lake of the Dead* and a cover like this one, it must be a *horror* novel, not a *crime* one, right?' The short answer is that it's a bit of both. To the extent that it involves a mysterious death and the efforts of the dead man's friends to investigate the matter and get to the bottom of it, it unquestionably follows the structure of a crime or mystery novel. And yet many of the specific plot points of the book – an abandoned cabin in the woods, a century-old curse, possession by an evil spirit, a lake with the paranormal power to suck victims down to their doom in its bottomless depths, a dead man said to return from beyond the grave – are much more closely aligned with the horror genre. It's worth noting that Bjerke wasn't the only author of the period to explore the possibilities of fusing crime and horror. Agatha Christie's *And Then There Were None* (1939) reads for all the world like a supernatural horror novel until a rational explanation is finally presented at the end, while John Dickson Carr took the opposite approach in *The Burning Court* (1937), offering a controversial twist ending that suggested a supernatural solution to the mystery. Bjerke knew both authors' works well (indeed both are mentioned explicitly by name in *The Lake of the Dead*), and he knew the possibilities and risks of introducing the supernatural into a mystery novel. To find out which approach Bjerke ultimately follows – a supernatural explanation or a rationalized one – you'll have to read the book.

If Norwegian critics have typically overlooked the book's supernatural or horror aspects and focused on the book only as a crime novel, it may be because (as discussed in the first volume of our *The Valancourt Book of World Horror Stories*) Norway is one of the only Western European countries with essentially no tradition of horror fiction. In the 1970s, when horror was booming worldwide, with hit books and films like Ira Levin's *Rosemary's Baby*, Thomas Tryon's *The Other*, and William Peter Blatty's *The Exorcist*, one Norwegian publisher thought to capitalize on the current appetite for horror and enlisted (who else?) André Bjerke, Norway's closest thing to a horror author, to edit two volumes of horror stories, one from Norway and the other from the rest of the world. The international book proved to be no problem for Bjerke – it came out in

1975 and contained most of the usual suspects, including Poe, M. R. James, Algernon Blackwood, and Conan Doyle; Bjerke even translated many of the tales into Norwegian himself. The second book, an anthology of Norwegian horror, was trickier. In fact, Bjerke recounts in the foreword that he had misgivings about the assignment because he thought the material was too scant. In the end he did manage to compile a slim volume of Norwegian horror, though he helped himself by padding out the page count with one story of his own, two by his father, and a translation of 'William and Mary' by British author Roald Dahl, whose parents happened to be Norwegian. Given that Norway has virtually no horror fiction to speak of, it would be fair to say that *The Lake of the Dead*, although typically classified as a crime novel, is one of the closest things to a horror novel to be found there.

But to pigeonhole Bjerke as merely a genre writer, an author of popular thrillers, would be a mistake. During his lifetime he was arguably better known for his poetry than his novels. His first collection came out in 1940 when he was only 22 and earned wide acclaim; he would go on to publish well over a dozen more volumes of verse for adults and children throughout his career and is still highly regarded for his achievements today. Proficient in English, French, and German, Bjerke was also a prolific translator, bringing many of the world's classics to Norwegian audiences, including Shakespeare, Goethe, Molière, Racine, Poe, Kipling, Hesse and Rilke, just to name a few. He was an extremely cultured and well-read man – as readers will see from the many erudite allusions to be found in *The Lake of the Dead*.

After the Nazis occupied Norway in June 1940, Bjerke made the leap from poetry to thrillers. This may have been in part because of financial considerations – after all, writing popular novels has almost always paid better than poetry – or perhaps the extremely creative young Bjerke wanted to try another outlet for expressing his ideas. Or it might simply have had to do with the fact that poetry, with its inherent ability to contain hidden layers of meaning, would have had a harder time getting past the German censors.

Like his contemporary Graham Greene, who distinguished between his more serious novels and his thrillers (which he labeled 'entertainments'), Bjerke sought to put some distance between his poetry and his genre fiction, publishing the latter under the pseudonym of 'Bernhard Borge'. His first novel, *Nattmennesket*, which translates literally as *The Night Person,* appeared when he was just 23; it would be the first of four novels published under the Borge moniker. In an early example of what we might call metafiction, Borge is presented not only as the author of Bjerke's novel, but also its main character: the tale is recounted in the first person by a middling crime author named Bernhard Borge. The trustworthiness of Borge's account is emphasized by his surname, which is a verb in Norwegian meaning 'to guarantee' or 'to vouch for'. Though no knowledge of the first book is necessary to understand and enjoy *The Lake of the Dead* (the novels are both stand-alone stories), it might be worth giving a brief summary of it here, since not much information about it is available in English.

Bjerke's debut novel opens with Bernhard Borge traveling to a weekend house party at the home of his uncle, Helge Gårholm, a notorious womanizer who adheres to the philosophy of 'love 'em and leave 'em' – his favorite pastime is to make women fall in love with him, then dump them flat and break their hearts. In addition to his nephew, Helge has invited a few male friends and several beautiful women, including his current fling and his most recent ex. In the course of the night, he is found murdered,

his throat slashed and his head nearly sawed off by a ser-
rated knife. A detective from Oslo named Hammer – no
relation to Mickey Spillane's Mike Hammer, who wouldn't
debut until six years later – arrives to investigate the
murder with a friend in tow, the psychiatrist Kai Bugge.
The two of them have a longstanding bet: Bugge believes
that he can solve a murder with his knowledge of Freudian
psychology faster than Hammer can with his policeman's
bag of tricks, such as tracking down alibis or dusting for
fingerprints. Bugge, incidentally, is based on a real person,
Trygve Braatøy (1904-1953), a psychiatrist known primarily
for introducing Sigmund Freud's theories into Norwegian
academia and for his study of Knut Hamsun's fiction
based on Freudian psychoanalysis. Bugge, we're told, has
a fashionable Oslo psychiatry practice treating hysterical
middle-aged women, but his true interest is in putting his
theoretical knowledge to the test in the world of crime
detection. The prime suspect in the case is Helge's ex,
a young woman named Sonja (when we meet her again
in *The Lake of the Dead*, she'll be married to Bernhard and
raising two children). After a number of clues and red her-
rings, the real murderer is of course finally revealed, and
unlike in *The Lake of the Dead*, no trace of the supernatural
is to be found.

It's an enjoyable book, what's sometimes called a
'cozy crime' novel, since Hammer and Bugge's constant
presence in the house after the corpse is discovered fairly
assures no further murders will take place, meaning there's
no particular sense of threat or unease, just a wait for the
eventual unmasking. But although it can still be read with
pleasure today, to a certain extent *Nattmennesket* reads like
what it is – a first novel by a young man who has read a lot
of Agatha Christie.

In the single year that elapses between this book and *The
Lake of the Dead*, Bjerke advances light years as a novelist:

his second effort is considerably more suspenseful and compulsively page-turning; if you didn't know it had been written by a young man of 24, you would assume from its assured tone and masterful pacing that it was the work of a mature writer at the height of his powers. Published in 1942, again under the Borge pseudonym, Bjerke's book became an instant hit and has rarely, if ever, been out of print in Norway. At its most basic level, it's a book about a mysterious death and an attempt to find an explanation for it, whether suicide, murder, or something paranormal. But the book can also be read more broadly as dealing with a central conflict: modern-day science and rationalism versus age-old belief in the occult and supernatural.

This is not, of course, a new theme in literature; it wasn't even new when Marie Corelli tackled the same issue in *The Sorrows of Satan* (1895) decades earlier. Corelli's book is set in modern-day London, where a new creed of materialism has replaced a belief in God, making the city fertile ground for the Devil when he returns in the guise of a fashionable prince. Many of the arguments employed by Bjerke's character Gabriel Mørk, a fervent believer in the occult and supernatural, echo ones to be found in Corelli's novel half a century earlier. It's surprising, then, to see a novel published as late as 1942 covering much of the same ground in the science vs. spiritualism debate that had raged decades before. After all, one would think that the airy and ethereal world of the supernatural would be the farthest thing from people's minds in 1942, when there were considerably more down-to-earth problems to worry about. Norway was occupied by the Nazis and Norwegians were enduring rationing, shortages, and other daily hardships, while elsewhere in the world the war was being waged fiercely and real-life horrors were being perpetrated in concentration camps.

But the fact that Bjerke treats the supernatural as a

serious topic of debate in 1942 is perhaps less surprising if we take into account a strange event that happened in Norway in the 1930s. Ludwig Dahl, a judge and mayor of Bergen, was a fervent believer in spiritualism and regularly conducted seances, believing it was a means of communicating with his two deceased sons, who had died tragically in accidents at young ages. During one seance in 1933, the medium claimed to have a message for Dahl from his son Ragnar, saying that Dahl would perish in August of the following year. When August 1934 came around, Dahl was visiting the seaside at the same spot where his son had drowned fifteen years earlier. An expert swimmer, Dahl ventured out into the water, where he was suddenly sucked down beneath the surface and drowned. The prophecy from the great beyond had been fulfilled. Or perhaps not: as it turned out, Dahl's family was in desperate financial straits, and he had a lucrative life insurance policy that was set to expire the very next day. The daughter – and the medium – were charged with a plot to murder him for the insurance money; the court proceedings went on for three years and became an international sensation. Science was literally pitted against spiritualism in a court of law – Norwegians and the rest of the world were captivated. In the end, the verdict was acquittal, and Dahl's death to this day is officially classified as an accident, but not all believers in the occult are convinced. Considering Bjerke mentions Dahl by name in the novel, and given the visual imagery of his being sucked down to his death in a body of water, it's hard to imagine the case wasn't in the author's mind when formulating his book.

In *The Lake of the Dead*, the psychiatrist Bugge is the spokesman for the modern-day belief that there's a rational explanation for everything, and that all things in the universe are governed by natural, scientific laws. His friend, the literary critic Mørk (whose surname appropriately means 'dark' in Norwegian), takes the opposite stance, believing that the twentieth century has been too quick to jettison belief in God and the Devil; in short, he subscribes to Hamlet's view about there being 'more things in Heaven and Earth than are dreamt of in [our] philosophy'. Mørk's mind is made up at the beginning of the novel: he's convinced an occult phenomenon is at work. But Bugge, the sober-minded medical professional, can't or won't accept such a hypothesis and spends the rest of the novel trying to find an alternative explanation. The oft-cited principle of Occam's razor teaches us that when faced with two possible solutions to a problem, we should accept the simplest. As you read the book, you'll have to consider for yourself which man's theories about the case are ultimately the most far-fetched.

In addition to this debate between the material and spiritual views of the world, the author's daughter, Vilde Bjerke, has seen another dimension in the novel. She argues that the book includes symbolism that makes it a subtly anti-Nazi text. In her view, the lake, with its deadly attractive properties, represents the sinister allure of Nazi ideology, while the character of Liljan, the pure, lily-white young woman, represents Norway, which the male characters, a sort of group of resistance fighters, must try to save. Whether Bjerke intended such a reading or not, the fact that the book is open to additional layers of interpretation is further testament to how much more serious a literary effort his book is than most other crime novels of the period.

One other aspect of the novel bears mentioning here. A number of Norwegian readers, reviewing the book online, have commented that although it's a first-rate thriller, their enjoyment of the story was hampered by what they see as its misogyny. This doesn't seem an entirely accurate criticism. Misogyny, after all, is defined as a hatred of women (from the Greek *miso-*, hatred + *gyne*, woman), and I don't think any fair reading of the book would conclude that it shows a hatred of women. Indeed, at one point in the novel Bjerke explicitly notes that one of the characters (the occultist Mørk) is a misogynist, thus implying that, in his view at least, the other characters – and himself – are not. However, there's no denying that the book's attitude towards women seems very dated in 2021. The novel has paternalistic and chauvinistic tendencies that some readers may find off-putting. Women are described on a number of occasions as the 'weaker sex' and as fragile beings in need of the male characters' protection, and Bernhard's wife, Sonja, spends the greater part of the book in the background, her role limited to making coffee and food for the male characters and looking attractive in a bathing suit. Meanwhile, most of the real action in the novel is reserved to the men, who also spend a lot of time smoking and drinking while the women toil in the kitchen. For the most part, though, although the depiction of gender roles in the book feels dated, I'm not sure it's actually all that offensive; in fact, at times it's so over the top as to be almost unintentionally humorous. It should go without saying, but before we cast stones at Bjerke for his portrayal of gender roles, it bears remembering that the book was written eighty years ago, when men and women's societal roles were often regarded much differently than today. It's also worth noting in passing that Sonja is described by several of the male characters as 'brave', in explicit contrast to her cowardly husband, and towards the end of the book, while Bernhard is still flailing around in hopeless incomprehension of what is going on, Sonja is taking bold and decisive action to bring the climax to a head. Ultimately, as a spine-chilling thriller, the book is timeless; hopefully readers will overlook a few moments in it that may feel a little dated.

After the success of *The Lake of the Dead*, it would be five more years before the next 'Bernhard Borge' novel hit bookstore shelves. Why? Vilde Bjerke explains that during the Nazi occupation publishers were not only subject to censorship; in some cases they were actually co-opted by the Germans to be instruments of propaganda and profit to the Nazi cause. Bjerke, a fervent anti-Nazi who had taken part in the Norwegian resistance, refused to participate in anything that could aid the Germans in any way and abstained from publishing until after they were finally forced out of Norway in 1945.

In 1947, then, the third novel appears under the Borge pseudonym, *Døde menn går i land* [*Dead Men Go Ashore*]. By then Bjerke's authorship of the novels was the Norwegian publishing world's worst-kept secret, but he retained the pseudonym all the same. This time, though, the pseudonym hides two authors: for the first time Bjerke worked with a co-author, the crime novelist Bjørn Carling. It's the only one of the four 'Borge' novels not to feature Kai Bugge, but otherwise it repeats the recipe for success from *The Lake of the Dead*, mixing the supernatural and crime to great effect. In the preface to the most recent Norwegian reprint, the author Knut Nærum describes it as 'one of the most exciting books written in Norwegian'. (It's a testimony to the enduring popularity of Bjerke's work that Nærum has also published successful parodies of it, including *De dødes båt* (2008) [*The Boat of the Dead*], a send-up of *The Lake of the Dead* – after all, imitation is the sincerest form of flattery!)

A fourth novel, *Skjult mønster* [*Hidden Pattern*], featuring the return of Kai Bugge, appeared in 1950. It would be the last appearance of Bjerke's famous psychiatrist detective. Bjerke claimed that he 'got tired of him', but Carling suggests there might have been more to it than that. In his view, Bjerke began to find Bugge's dogged belief that

there was a rational explanation for everything to be problematic; as the author got older, he increasingly came to
believe that there were phenomena and forces, both within
human beings and in the world around them, that science
did not and could not understand.

Which brings us to an interesting later work by Bjerke,
Enhjørningen [*The Unicorn*] (1963). The book opens with a
frame narrative, in which four men – a journalist, a writer,
a businessman, and a psychiatrist – are playing cards, drinking, and talking. The conversation turns to the theme of
the supernatural and inexplicable, and then each of the
characters takes turns telling stories of experiences from
his life which he believes to provide evidence of the paranormal. The psychiatrist – like Bugge in Bjerke's earlier
works – believes only in science, and after each man fin-
ishes telling his story, he sets out to debunk it meticulously,
demonstrating how what seemed to be an otherworldly
phenomenon could actually be explained scientifically. But
what's telling is that as the book goes on, the explanations
become more and more absurd. At some point, it becomes
not only simpler, but actually *more probable*, to believe in
the supernatural explanation – it's the only one that really
makes sense. Thus the debate between Mørk and Bugge
from *The Lake of the Dead* is played out again in even starker
terms; if a young Bjerke felt that the existence of the occult
and paranormal was a matter for honest debate, by later in
his career he seems fully convinced of its reality. Even later
in life, Bjerke would co-host the first Norwegian television
series dedicated to the paranormal, *Streiftog i grenseland*
[*Expedition to the Borderland*] (1971-72); episodes covered
topics like ghosts, flying saucers, and the Loch Ness monster.

The Lake of the Dead was adapted for a film version,
released in 1958 and directed by Kåre Bergstrøm. Not
satisfied with merely having written one of the all-time

best Norwegian thrillers, Bjerke also co-wrote the script for the film version, which became the first Norwegian horror film and has gone on to be considered one of the best Norwegian films ever made. There's nothing new, of course, about novelists making the transition to film, but Bjerke took it to a whole new level, not only co-writing the screenplay, but actually *co-starring* in the film. Curiously, though, he doesn't portray his famous psychiatrist-detective Bugge, nor the book's narrator Borge; instead, he plays the role of the occultist Gabriel Mørk. No doubt it was just a casting decision, but one is tempted to read into it a sense of Bjerke's identification with Mørk's views on the paranormal. A fun trivia fact: during the filming of *The Lake of the Dead*, Bjerke and the actress playing Liljan, Henny Moan, fell in love; the two married and had a daughter, Vilde, who has written a memoir of her father and has spent many years championing his work and reputation.

The film was a substantial success (there are even anecdotal reports, which I've so far been unable to verify, that the film was so terrifying to Norwegian audiences at the time that some viewers had to leave the theater). Certainly it holds up today as an extremely atmospheric horror film; a recent review by the English critic Kim Newman likens it to classics by William Castle and Val Lewton, while also seeing parallels to the chilling masterpiece *The Innocents* (1961). At the time of writing, a decent quality bootleg with English subtitles was available from the mail-order company Sinister Cinema. A less successful and less intelligent remake appeared in 2019 and is currently available to watch on the streaming service Shudder under the title *Lake of Death*.

This new Valancourt edition marks the first appearance of Bjerke's book in America, but it had a short-lived existence in England in 1961, when the publisher Macdonald released it in hardcover under the title *Death in the Blue Lake*.

The print run seems to have been very small; the book is held at only a couple of libraries worldwide and is totally unobtainable on the secondhand market. The translation, though written in a fluid and highly readable mid-20th-century British style, suffers from a number of issues, including misreadings and omissions throughout, as well as a fair amount of rather liberal paraphrasing. Names in particular pose a problem. The ominously suggestive 'Dead Man's Cabin', for example, becomes the decidedly unthreatening 'Daumann's Hut'. Some of the names are anglicized (Liljan / Lilian, Sonja / Sonia, Harald / Harold), which isn't a major problem (though one wonders how Bernhard escaped being rechristened 'Bernard'), but other changes are more problematic. Bjørn, whose name is also the Norwegian word for *bear*, becomes 'Teddy', and the lawyer Gran, whose surname means *spruce*, is changed to Tann, the German word for *fir*. (If 'Spruce' seems an unlikely last name, keep in mind how many trees there are in Norway; Bjerke's own name derives from the Norwegian word for 'birch'). The explanation for the various bizarre aspects of the translation seems to be that, despite the title page's statement that it is 'translated from the Norwegian', the book is actually based on the 1949 German edition, *Tod im Blausee*. Thus, it's a translation of a translation, and what's more, based on an outdated version of the text, since Bjerke had revised the book in the 1950s for the film tie-in edition. The present edition, then, is the first complete translation of Bjerke's preferred text to appear in English.

As mentioned above, Bjerke is an extremely allusive writer. Peppered throughout *The Lake of the Dead* are references to Norwegian literature in particular, but also American, British, French, and German writers and works, as well as biblical citations, and a couple of German phrases. I've reluctantly included a small number of endnotes (marked in the text with an asterisk) in cases where a reference seemed likely to escape most modern readers. Not one of the endnotes is absolutely essential to an understanding of the story, so readers who wish to devour the book without interruption needn't feel obliged to pause their reading and flip to the back of the book.

The Lake of the Dead may not be a flawless novel (how many novels are?), but even now, eighty years since its first publication, it remains an extremely gripping, genuinely creepy and atmospheric read with enough twists, turns, and surprises to enthrall even the most jaded of modern readers. We here at Valancourt think it's a important rediscovery that deserves a place on any list of the best Golden Age thrillers. So, without further ado, readers, it's time to pack your bags and set out for a little holiday at Dead Man's Cabin. Don't mind the creaks coming from the floorboards in the next room or the bone-chilling screams you hear outside the cabin. You'll be fine. Maybe just don't go for a swim in the lake . . .

JAMES D. JENKINS
Richmond, Virginia
June 30, 2021

JAMES D. JENKINS is the co-founder of Valancourt Books and the co-editor of the multi-award-nominated *The Valancourt Book of World Horror Stories* and the four volumes of the acclaimed *The Valancourt Book of Horror Stories* series. A polyglot, he reads over twenty languages and has published translations of stories from over a dozen of these. Recently one of his translations from *The Valancourt Book of World Horror Stories, vol. 1* was a finalist for the Shirley Jackson Award and two others were chosen for inclusion in *The Rosetta Archive*, an anthology of the best translated speculative fiction of 2020.

CHAPTER ONE

In which I have a bad case of writer's block

THERE'S A GOOD, OLD RULE that says you should begin at the beginning. When women tell a story, they usually start with the point of it – assuming it has a point, which most often it doesn't. We men, on the other hand, the factual-minded sex, know how to tell a story properly: we always start at the beginning. And the starting point for the series of events related here dates back to one evening late last summer. The 30th of July, 1941, to be precise.

Sonja and I had just taken possession of our lovely new apartment on Kirkevei, and we had decided to celebrate the occasion by throwing a little party for our friends. We had originally planned on just having three or four people over for a simple, intimate little housewarming. The funny thing is that when word of something like that gets around, it suddenly turns out you have twice as many friends as at any other time. A number of people from the periphery of my circle of acquaintances rushed to congratulate us on finally having a decent roof over our heads – and then invited themselves to a cozy little party under that same roof. Sonja's cooking is famous all over town, and Bernhard Borge has always been a man with a big heart, so it wound up being a real crowd.

The first two years of our marriage Sonja and I had lived in one of the modern cubbyholes down on Wergelandsvei. You know, one of those charmingly tiny apartments where the kitchen is so small that you have to go out and come back in again every time you want to turn around. You can be as snug in a place like that as – quite literally – a bug in a rug, but when Sonja gave birth to our second son – reproduction at Japanese tempo* – we had to look for something with a little more breathing room. Around that time, one of my wife's distant cousins had begun to suffer from the so-called *ennui* that's supposedly so common in big cities. He wanted to go back to nature and live off the land, or something like that. Sonja and I immediately capitalized on his romantic weakness, taking over his co-op apartment at a ridiculously low price. Which was of course a good reason for a big celebration.

As usual, Sonja proved to be a born hostess. In the first three hours of the party, she conjured up incalculable quantities of oxtail soup, lobster, roast goose, mushrooms, and strawberries. Several bottles of choice champagne were drunk 'as the desert drinks summer rain', to quote Linklater,* and we had just launched a major offensive on the cognac. The mood was already at heights rarely seen since the good old days. However, if you want an explanation for these culinary excesses, I'm afraid I don't know what to tell you. That sort of thing is, and remains, my wife's secret; it's one of the mysteries that won't be cleared up in the following chapters, no doubt one of the book's shortcomings as a crime novel.

There were ten of us gathered around that cheerful table: first of all Sonja and I, each reigning over our respective ends of the table, then Kai Bugge, Gabriel Mørk, Harald Gran, and Bjørn Werner and his sister Liljan. There were also three young ladies whose names I don't need to mention, since they play no further role in this story, and since in this chapter they prudently follow Paul's excellent precept about women keeping quiet in company.* Let me go ahead and introduce the characters in my drama so that they won't just seem a big blur to the reader; after all, it has to be done sooner or later, so I might as well jump right in.

I'll start with Kai Bugge. He needs no introduction; those who have read my book on the Gårholm case have already gotten an excellent picture of him,* and of course the cultured reading public knows him from his extensive writings on psychoanalysis. It's common knowledge that his scientific ideas trickle out onto the book market at short intervals – usually as collections of essays written in a smooth and ironic style, with sharp polemical jabs at both the right and the left. Most men find him unbearably arrogant and conceited, but on the other hand he has an improbably good grasp of women. The results of his psychoanalysis with women in the 'dangerous age' (26-50 years) are remarkable, and a number of husbands here in Oslo have complained about their wives becoming disturbingly passionate after going through Bugge's treatment. At the public library you'll find a number of his books filled with enthusiastic penciled comments from ladies of all ages who have felt their minds liberated by their reading. Personally I like Bugge well enough, despite his penchant for putting me in my place every time he gets the chance, and even though I can't bring myself to share his viewpoints in any way; they seem strange and twisted to me. But he's a man who goes his own way, just like Kipling's cat. It's something I've always admired; I've invariably followed the herd.

Gabriel Mørk is a literary critic by profession. He edits a magazine called *The Scourge,* where once a month he excoriates everything trying to pass itself off as literature. In his view, modern literary criticism is all a big, brazen swindle, a hoax perpetrated by the shameless and talentless. Therefore he sees it as his mission in life to slander as many writers as possible and smite the sewers of intellectual life like God's cleansing thunderbolt. In most respects he's Bugge's diametric opposite: he nurtures a sublime contempt for everything that smacks of natural science and rationalism;

his interests lean strongly towards the occult and super-natural. Mørk and Bugge are continually at each other's throats; they keep each other on their toes with a crossfire of ironic remarks and never miss an opportunity to mock each other's beliefs. In other words, they are inseparable friends.

Harald Gran is a lawyer, which should be enough for the reader to lose all interest in him. But Gran isn't your usual ambulance chaser. Ever since reading 'The Mystery of Marie Roget' by flashlight under his blanket at the age of nine, he has been strongly drawn towards criminology. Like the bright and energetic young mind he is, he rejected the idea of joining his father's law firm with proud scorn and tried to set up a private detective practice instead. But that career turned out to have little or none of the roman-tic aura of crime fiction about it. After a full year in prac-tice, Gran had handled fourteen cases: two bicycle thefts, a search for a lost Pekinese, three cases of garden variety persecution mania, and finally eight instances of women past their prime who wanted to know if their husbands were committing adultery when they were supposed to be at board meetings. As might be expected, Gran found it beneath his scientific dignity to continue in that line of work, and he resigned himself to the world of business. But he still cherishes his love for his old hobby, and for the past couple of years he's been busy writing a long crim-inological thesis that he keeps shrouded in the greatest secrecy. On that point, incidentally, his and Bugge's inter-ests coincide; Bugge's masterpiece is *Das Verbrechen als Erlösung*,* a grotesque and unreadable book published in Vienna in 1932.

What exactly Bjørn Werner does is a little harder to make out. He started by studying theology, but like all theologians he became a confirmed atheist after six months and turned instead to literature and languages.

He has carefully avoided taking any exams, claiming that sort of thing only blunts your abilities; what's more, by taking exams you risk the worst fate of all: namely, getting a steady job. Thanks to the conveniently timed death of a rich uncle, Werner can allow himself the luxury of being a slacker; the only thing he's managed to squeeze out as far as I know is a sort of essay on 'The Significance of Beatrice in Dante's Poetry', a subject he finds interesting, oddly enough. In terms of appearance, there is still a certain something 'theological' about him: a narrow, bony face with ascetic features, long, thin limbs that give an almost insect-like impression, and finally a body that inevitably makes you think of one of the old martyrs. But even if you might say his appearance is against him to a certain degree, he's a likable guy. I've always had a soft spot for people who aren't cut out to amount to anything in this world.

His sister Liljan is totally different, almost the prototype of the modern young woman, a little too nervous and a little too erotic; you'll find her described in Gyldendal's series of modern novels, volumes 1 to 52.* Her appearance reminds me a little of Sonja's, but my wife is of course much sweeter and gentler. Liljan has something hard about her, something 'unresolved', as they say in books; I can't quite put my finger on what it is. Every so often, though, she'll get a strange twinkle in her eye, and then as a rule I make sure to stay far away. You never know what one of those twinkles can lead to, and I have a terrible weakness for them. I'm a married man, after all, and should keep the old scripture in mind: 'Anyone who looks at a woman . . .' etc.* Incidentally, Sonja and Liljan are best friends and stick together constantly like Siamese twins.

In the course of an hour the traditional speeches were made. Bugge opened with an address to the hosts, a chivalrous distribution of insults to me and compliments to Sonja. Next Bjørn Werner delivered an address to Woman, a subject he knows absolutely nothing about and on which he can therefore express his views with all the more authority. Then came Gabriel Mørk, with a spiritual and fiery speech about his magazine, that last bulwark of humanity, that stronghold of the spirit, where he, the last crusader, fights his battle against darkness with the sharp blade of the word. Finally Harald Gran talked about the new apartment, this beautiful and worthy environment for Bernhard Borge's rising star, this writer's home *par excellence*, this modern-day Aulestad.* Gone were the days when writers had to live in garrets and barrels, gone were the days when tuberculosis and threadbare pants were prerequisites for intellectual life. Henceforth artists would have their share of life's riches – why should those riches be reserved only for the dim-witted bourgeoisie? In this new home, I, Bernhard Borge, would be newly inspired; in this Parnassian air I would manufacture – he used the word 'manufacture' – a dozen more crime novels for the intellectual benefit of my people and for the material benefit of myself, my wife, my children, and – last but not least – my friends and acquaintances.

Everyone agreed this was a fine speech and that it set the mood for the occasion. But strangely enough, as he spoke I felt more and more oppressed by the pangs of a guilty conscience. It was a feeling that had plagued me since the morning we moved into the apartment, but I had suppressed it, to put it in Bugge's jargon. Now suddenly I couldn't hold it back any longer; it blazed out.

I realized the others were looking at me, clearly they were expecting the host to say a few words. All at once I felt a strong and immediate need to unburden myself and tapped my champagne glass with my fork.

'The leader of the Kristiania Bohemians,* Bernhard Borge, has the floor,' said Werner, in his self-appointed role as master of ceremonies.

I stood up. I noticed that the drinks were already having their effect; the parquet floor had started to rock beneath me. But I managed at once to strike the proper oratorical pose, the upright, freestanding posture that Cicero must have adopted at the Forum when he made his speeches against Verres.

'Ladies and gentlemen,' I said. 'The last esteemed speaker gave beautiful and sensitive lyrical expression to what all of us think about material possessions, and he also emphasized the legitimate claim we – er – intellectuals have to lead lives of beauty, if I may put it like that. As for my own modest self, I have every reason to be thankful for the generosity of Providence. So far Fortune's gods have smiled on me: the gods of the reading public, of the publishing industry, of the newspapers and magazines. I've enjoyed a totally undeserved success, and everything I've touched has turned – if not to gold – at least to nice, fat piles of banknotes. But as my great predecessor Goethe used to say – or maybe it was Schiller (I'm afraid I can't keep those two old fellows straight, since I've never read either of them) – *"Des Lebens ungemischte Freude ward keinem Irdischen zuteil."** The only question is: *how long will it last?*

'Have you, ladies and gentlemen, ever tried to imagine what it means to earn your living from crime fiction? Do you know it's like building your house on quicksand? A crime writer has to be as fertile as an African jungle, he must be able to produce like a rabbit in the summer heat, he must be as bottomless as the Widow of Zarephath's jug.* If he relaxes for a single instant, if he loses his grip for just one second on that great, greedy monster, *the reading public*, then he's finished – his sales plunge and he inevitably ends up in the poorhouse. Do you think that we who write for the masses, we outsiders to intellectual life, are better off than the so-called "real" writers? Just the opposite. I admit that a lyric poet, for example, may starve to death because he writes verses that millions of traveling salesmen, maids, waiters, and plumbers don't understand a word of. Quite true. Yet he dies in beauty, with grape leaves in his hair. Posterity will remember him, literary history will sprinkle its dust on him, and children will be forced to memorize him in school. But when one of *us* perishes, we literary mayflies, he just slips into the gray fog of anonymity, into the shadowy world of oblivion. We are children of the present, we write for the present, and we die with the present. The fact that we don't set our sights on eternity means we have to struggle ten times harder for survival. Our audience is extremely forgetful, which is why we constantly have to watch over our star so it doesn't burn out in the heavens. I often think there's something almost heroic about this profession I've chosen . . .'

I stood there, suddenly aware that I had in fact been unusually eloquent. The words formed in my mouth almost miraculously, shaping themselves dutifully into quick, nimble sentences. Maybe I needed to get it all out. Or maybe it was the alcohol. I could feel it tingling in my body; it was like an army of little ants stampeding through my nerves, cascading out in a cheerful swarm towards my fingertips, to settle down there and rub their antennae against my skin.

'To get to the point,' I continued. 'I've taken a look at my financial situation today. On the debit side, there are a number of things: in the first place, my personal consumption, which I think old Lucullus would have envied; secondly, this apartment, whose rent, just between us, is astronomical; third, my children, who eat their weight in food every day and cost a fortune in diapers, toys, and pacifiers; finally, my wife, the apple of my eye, the jewel of my soul, who these past few years has managed to keep my wallet just as slim as her own lovely body.' (Here Sonja interrupted, protesting indignantly.) 'On the credit side are the books and short stories I've had the privilege to write over time, and in addition, the books and short stories that will – and must! – issue from my pen in the future. Which brings us to the point, ladies and gentlemen, the tragic point that is making me look to the future with dread. I've concluded today that I have nothing left to write about. I'm totally out of material – my pen has dried up – I've got writer's block. Ladies and gentlemen, I have sad news for you: as of 12:00 today, Bernhard Borge is washed up; I'm as empty as the fleshpots of our time . . .'*

I paused and looked around the room with a gloomy expression. Bugge and Gran broke into hearty laughter almost simultaneously, and Mørk raised his glass to me from across the table.

'Congratulations,' he said. 'You've finally made an observation I can tip my hat to.'

'So, as you'll understand,' I continued, 'the sword of Damocles is already hanging menacingly over my head; the specter of a death by starvation is knocking at my door with its bony hand. Therefore I'll conclude with an appeal to my esteemed guests: give me an idea, give me a plot! If you can't – or won't – help me now, I can only warn you that the next party I'll throw for you will be held at the homeless shelter. Cheers, ladies and gentlemen!'

There was a pause for a few seconds after my speech. It wasn't really what they had expected to hear. They had anticipated a loftier address, a more cheerful outlook on life, when Bernhard Borge went to the podium for once. I sat down.

'And now I'd love to hear your suggestions,' I said. 'All contributions gratefully received.'

'Take it easy,' Werner suggested. 'Do like Mr Micawber; put your feet up on the table and wait for something to turn up.'

'That contribution will be returned to sender,' I said.

'Can't use it. After all, it's what you've been doing your whole life, and we can all see how that's turned out. As for me, I've had my feet up on the table for fourteen days now, and I'm starting to find the position untenable. Come up with something better, gentlemen! What do you suggest, Bugge?'

Bugge removed the cigarette from the corner of his mouth and blew out a large, fleecy cumulus cloud.

'Well, I must admit you've really gone downhill lately, Bernhard. Your stories are starting to remind me more and more of the run-of-the-mill stuff you see in boys' magazines. But if you're tired of writing obscure literature, why not let someone else do it for you? Start a novel factory, get some people to build your books like they'd build a tunnel. Have one person start from the beginning of the book and another from the end, and make sure they meet in the middle. Before long you'll outpace Stein Riverton,* who incidentally worked in exactly the same way. Division of labor is the modern-day solution.'

I folded my hands across my chest.

'My pride forbids me from resorting to unworthy means,' I said. 'The Borge family can trace its roots back to the fifteenth century, and our coat of arms, which depicts a leaping wolf and a lily, bears the motto: Be bold! Be pure!'

'Then you should quit writing books,' Mørk declared, setting his champagne glass down heavily, but without managing to break the stem. 'Quit writing books, that's my advice. Modern books are mental fornication, a profanation of the Word, the Holy Word, which was there in the beginning. When John of Patmos writes about the great whore in the Book of Revelation, there's no doubt he had our contemporary literature in mind.'

'Then what do you expect me to do?'

'Look inside yourself and try to develop your consciousness. Recognize that you're the product of an empty and vulgar age, a mass-produced article, a child of Ford. Recognize that the material world is an illusion, an underworld, inorganic like the minerals it's made of. Try to rise from the dead, try to recognize that the only real life is the life of the *spirit*. Join a monastery or dig yourself a hole in the earth like the fakirs do, but whatever you do, quit writing books!'

Here Mørk slammed his champagne glass down on the table again, and this time the stem did break.

Bugge laughed.

'Don't listen to Mørk,' he said. 'He's poisoned by bitterness. He can't forget that he spent his youth writing poetry about death, so he's taking his revenge on life. Now he sits like a wrathful Jehovah in the clouds, smiting the Philistine armies with plagues. Have another drink, old friend, here's the cognac –'

'Kindly refrain from psychoanalyzing me,' Mørk exclaimed. 'Psychoanalyze yourself instead and those who think like you, in short, the whole spiritual vacuum of our time, but leave me alone. I think what I think, and it's all the same to me if, with the combined help of the materialistic view of history, the theory of relativity, and psychoanalysis, you discover that I have the basest motives. I despise modern intellectual life. Think of how many perfectly good Norwegian forests have been leveled so that books could be made out of them! Just think of a proud old tree in the woods, a giant fir with the wind rustling through its branches, a world in itself. And then one day some pygmy comes and cuts it down and sends it to Oslo to be turned into literature. Damn it, I say, damn it! One of these days I'll go down and plant a bomb under the Authors' Guild . . .'

Suddenly Gran raised his hand and snapped his fingers.

'I've got it!' he said.

'What have you got?' I looked at him expectantly.

'The material for your next book. Of course. My gosh, it's first-rate stuff. I'd almost like to use it myself.'

'For God's sake, spit it out.'

'I suggest we adjourn first and sit around the fire. A good story should be told in the right atmosphere. And this story demands very subdued lighting and a fire with large, crackling logs. It's a really creepy one.'

'Bravo!' I cried. 'Absolutely and definitely bravo! You're a peach, Gran. You warm the cockles of my heart. Let's leave the table at once, there's no need to thank us for the food. Wife, put on some coffee.'

We got up and began to assemble in the large, deep leather armchairs by the fire. I built up a splendid bonfire of pine logs, dimmed the lights, and settled into the largest and deepest chair. Sonja disappeared for a while, and when she came back you could hear the cozy sound of the coffee simmering in the kitchen.

'Well?' I said.

'Don't get your hopes up too much,' Gran said with a smile. 'Strictly speaking, what I have to tell isn't really a story, only the outline of one. You'll have to expand on it yourself.'

'Count on it.'

'All right. I thought of this when you used the phrase "the *specter* of a death by starvation".'

'Aha. In other words, it's a ghost story.'

'Exactly.'

'But that's all been done to death long ago. The classic in the genre is Sverre Vegenor's landmark work, "The Yellow Phantom", which appeared in *Detective Magazine*, number 14.'*

'Very possible. But I still think this one is a little out of the ordinary. It's really Werner who should be telling it, but I have more of a knack for storytelling, so it's better if I do it. So, then. Two weeks ago, our friend Werner bought an old cabin up in Østerdalen – '

'Oh, it's *that* story,' exclaimed Liljan Werner, who was chain-smoking cigarettes in the chair next to mine. The flames in the hearth cast a yellow glow on her sleek, silk-clad legs. 'Do you really have to tell that kind of thing now, when we're having such a nice time?'

'You've just heard that Bernhard's life and future are at stake,' said Gran. 'So let me get started. As I said, Werner has bought a cabin in the woods in Østerdalen, close to a little body of water called Blue Lake. It's one of the gloomiest and most godforsaken parts of the country, mile after mile of dense, black forest; the nearest inhabited spot is a little village, a hamlet about two hours from the cabin. Besides that, you might happen upon the occasional logger wandering around up there in the wilderness; there's a small river nearby, used during part of the summer to float logs down. The cabin has been empty for the past generation; it's over a hundred years old, and in recent years it's been badly run-down, but Werner has had some people there to fix it up, patch the roof and walls and so on, enough to keep even the most aggressive forces of nature out. Every child in those parts knows that cabin; it's been talked about as far back as anyone can remember. A legend has formed about it, and it's become a sort of Sleeping Beauty's castle in the local imagination. They call it "Dead Man's Cabin".'

'This sounds good,' I murmured. 'A great prelude. Keep going.'

'About a hundred years ago there lived a rich man down in the village, a man by the name of Tore Gruvik. He built that house up in the woods and used it mostly as a hunting lodge; every autumn he would stay up there alone. The villagers describe Tore Gruvik as a coarse and ruthless person, a man without conscience or scruples. He's supposed to have been brutal towards those who owed him money, and in fact towards all the little people he had in his power. They say he was built like a giant, with a wild and terrifying appearance, something between a highwayman and a pirate from Captain Morgan's day. Though maybe we shouldn't focus too much on such features; it's the sort of picture often painted by a person's enemies. Maybe he just had a strong and imposing personality. But in any event, the fact is that he was hated by almost everyone who knew him. They say there was only one person Tore Gruvik could tolerate having around him: his sister. Or rather, he didn't just tolerate her – he worshipped her with an almost unhealthy affection. They had lived together since their parents' death, and it looked as if the sister would never marry, even though she was almost thirty. Many people thought her brother wouldn't allow it.'

'You're being too long-winded,' Werner interrupted. 'Do you have to go into so much detail? Why not get straight to the point? Besides, several of us have already heard this tall tale before.'

'This isn't an ordinary story you'd find in a magazine, or a news item about a train accident,' Gran insisted. 'This is a novel, an ancient tragedy, and so the presentation requires details. Anyway, Bernhard needs them for his book.'

'Of course,' I said. 'Please don't interrupt the storyteller. Go on, Gran, you're under my personal protection.'

'One day a new farmhand turned up on Gruvik's farm. The story doesn't tell us his name, but he must have been a typical rural Casanova, a skirt-chaser who had a way with the ladies, and at the same time the kind of guy who might remind you of one of Hamsun's vagabonds.* He went from farm to farm around the country taking on work. Everywhere he went, he got the girls inside the barn with him as quickly as possible; once the barn door had closed behind them, there was no resisting him. And then there was nothing left to do but go on to the next farm and repeat the experiment there. Abortion wasn't so common back then, so he left a long trail of bastards in his wake, clearly marking for posterity the path he'd taken across the countryside.

'Enough about that. So one day he arrived at Gruvik's farm, and Tore's sister fell for him right away. She didn't have much experience with men, and in her first encounter with the forces of nature she was immediately swept off her feet. But he must have been unusually interested in her as well; contrary to his habit, he suggested that she elope with him. She couldn't refuse him; one night they ran off into the woods together and were gone. Gruvik found out a few hours later and was livid with rage, rather understandably. People had a sense of family honor in the old days, and that sister was his most precious possession. He took down his biggest and mightiest ax, sharpened it for a whole hour in the woodshed, and then set out after the fugitives.'

Gran paused for effect and lit another cigarette. The silence was broken only by the crackling sparks from the pine logs. I could see from the faces around me that the audience was starting to get caught up in the story. Even Mørk and Bugge evidently couldn't contain their interest.

'I can't believe you haven't told me this story before, Liljan,' said Sonja, almost reproachfully. 'I can't wait to see how it turns out. I kind of think I'm rooting for the two who ran off.'

'The two lovers made an unpardonable error,' Gran continued. 'They didn't count on Tore discovering their flight and coming after them that same night, and so they chose to spend the night at Gruvik's own cabin up in the woods. You might say that was a pretty stupid thing to do, but peasants live more in the moment than we city people and don't consider their actions as carefully as we do. Besides, there weren't too many empty hotel rooms in those parts, and "the ground was wet with dew", as Wildenvey says.* Meanwhile, Gruvik had an intuition that the presumptuous pair had sought refuge in his cabin; he went up there posthaste and caught them in the act. Tore Gruvik must have been a zealous man and thought that he who loves his sister should discipline her promptly,* so he chopped off both her head and her lover's and threw their bodies into Blue Lake.'

Instinctively I moved closer to the fire.

'But that deed was too great a strain even for a tough guy like Tore Gruvik. The next two days he wandered around restlessly in the forest, and on the third he went insane, just plain crazy. That day he followed his victims: his guilty conscience drove him to suicide and he drowned himself in Blue Lake. Another – and possibly less reliable – version of the story says the devil himself came for him that third day and took him down to Hell, which according to some local experts lies directly beneath that lake. Which explains the strange blue glow in the water; it's supposed to come from the eternal blue fire said to burn down there. The locals certainly aren't lacking in imagination. Popular superstition – '

'Don't talk about superstition in this case,' interrupted Mørk. 'It's modern materialism that's superstitious. The popular imagination draws on secret, occult sources, forgotten worlds of wisdom, kingdoms that are off-limits to those with narrow, mechanical ways of thinking. The average farmer knows far more about the spiritual world than twenty-seven university professors put together.'

'Were the bodies found?' I asked.

'No, they were never found. Blue Lake is said to be bottomless; those who drown in a lake like that one keep on sinking and sinking – down to the center of the earth, for all I know. I'm not an expert on that kind of thing. But now we come to the point. Popular superstition – sorry, Mørk – has added a juicy little postscript to the story: it claims that Tore Gruvik *returns from the dead*. Well, maybe that's not so remarkable; in the country about every other person returns after their death, and any halfway respectable farm has its resident ghost. But Tore Gruvik is no ordinary phantom; he doesn't manifest externally, in the outer world, clad in a sheet and with all the conventional trappings, bones, rusty chains, and so on. He shows himself – if you will – from within.'

'What's that supposed to mean?'

'The legend says a curse has hung over the cabin ever since Gruvik's death. Anyone who stays within its four walls falls victim to that curse. They become possessed by Gruvik's evil spirit – he comes to them at night, from within, like a terrible force sucking at their souls. He draws them to him, fills them with his own curse, his own madness; he sucks them all down with him into the lake.'

'No! Stop with this horrible story,' cried Liljan, sticking her fingers in her ears. 'I don't want to hear any more.'

'But *I* want to tell,' said Gran, smiling. 'Anyone who spends the night in the cabin, in other words, becomes possessed by a sort of suicidal mania. After a few days an unknown and intangible force compels them to drown themselves in the Blue Lake. During the last century, three people – two from Oslo – are said to have stayed at "Dead Man's Cabin" a few years apart, using it as a base for grouse hunting. All three disappeared up there, one after the other. One of them was found later; he had drowned himself in a shallow part of the lake where the bottom is fairly firm. I've personally talked to one of the man's descendants and know that the story jibes on this point. Maybe you can see why people in those parts avoid that house like the plague, and why it's sat unused for over a generation; they haven't even dared to tear it down. But then Bjørn Werner, the twentieth-century man, turns up, buys the old enchanted castle, and will travel there the day after tomorrow to put his nerves of steel and concrete to the test . . .'

'Not exactly for that reason,' Werner broke in, smiling. 'Those woods are the loveliest hunting grounds you could ask for, a wonderland for an old hunter and idler like me.

And the funny thing is, the area is as good as undiscovered, a patch of virgin wilderness, a remnant of Paradise Lost right in the heart of Norway. As long as I can be in a place like that with a shotgun, a dog, and a crate of good books, the world can go take a flying leap for all I care. And a couple of ghosts more or less will have a hard time destroying the idyll.'

I turned to Gran.

'So this is the material that you think . . .'

'Exactly. You should be able to make something out of that. Have your book take place up at that cabin, with ultramodern young people as your characters and that old legend as the background. Put these smooth, superficial stock characters and their shallow Oslo jargon in sharp relief against the horror and mystery of nature. Show how short the distance is from the polished veneer of civilization to the ancient fear just below the surface. Bring out the stark contrasts in the book's style and language; create a synthesis of Lill Herlofson Bauer* and Edgar Allan Poe . . .'

I nodded.

'A good idea, a great idea, but – '

'If you're not sure about the material, you can go up to the cabin yourself and see if you can experience the effects on your own body. Approach it like a true naturalist. Flaubert never put out a book before spending years researching every detail he wrote about.'

'Thanks, but I don't feel a burning desire to get to know any spirits, especially not Tore Gruvik, after hearing your description of him. I think I'd rather to stick to the material world.'

Mørk cleared his throat.

'The material world?' he said, looking darkly into the flames. 'The material world is an illusion.'

'Long live the material world,' I said, raising the bottle. 'Another glass of cognac, gentlemen?'

CHAPTER TWO

*In which a paper in Bugge's wallet and a notice in the
newspaper form the prelude to a drama*

THEY SAY THAT THE Norwegian writer Nils Collett
Vogt was woken up by his sister every morning with
the call, 'Nils! Get up and write!'

The result of which was that over the years Collett Vogt
became one of our most productive writers. I don't know
whether my wife has heard that story, but the fact remains
that on the morning of August 19, Sonja made use of the
same method.

'Bernhard! Get up and write!' said Sonja.

From deep, deep down in an impenetrable green darkness I slid slowly upwards towards the light of day, like a
pearl fisher after a dive among coral reefs.

'Aaaaaaaah,' I yawned, stretching as far as my silk pajamas would allow. 'What time is it, wife?'

'Half past twelve,' Sonja replied, looking at me accusingly. 'Don't you think a respectable person should be
awake by now?'

'I'm not a respectable person,' I declared. 'Besides, the
notion that you should get up in the morning is just an
old prejudice. All the important people in history have
gotten up after noon. The so-called circadian rhythm only
applies to those who work in places like offices and dairy
shops.'

Sonja ignored me. She turned to the mirror and considered her new summer dress with interest.

'Little wife,' I said. 'Sweet little wife, don't look so

grumpy. Come here now and give me my good-morning kiss before you bring me breakfast in bed!'

'You miserable good-for-nothing!' yelled Sonja. 'Here I am, wearing myself out with rehearsals at the theater night and day, while you just lie around like a blanket. How is your new novel coming along, anyway? Shouldn't it be done soon?'

'You're talking like my publisher instead of my heart's true love,' I said reprovingly. 'No, my new novel isn't finished, for the very good reason that I haven't started it yet.'

'You're lazy!'

'Agreed. I'm lazy. What is it the German philosopher Schlegel says? "Laziness is the virtue of genius, and idleness is the romantic ideal." '

'Get out of bed, or else – '

She stood over me with a pitcher of water.

'I'm coming, I'm coming!' I shouted in alarm. 'Good lord, why did I ever give up the bachelor life?'

*

'Any news?' I asked a few minutes later, when we were seated at the breakfast table and a little morning cocktail had lightened the mood. 'What's in today's announcements?'

'Harald Gran and Liljan Werner are engaged.'

'Really? I've suspected for quite a while there was something between them. Liljan gets so clumsy and awkward every time Harald's around. Are they planning a wedding?'

'I don't know, but they've moved into a studio apartment together at any rate.'

'Aha. You mean they're living in sin?'

'Exactly.' Sonja laughed. 'What's more, there's someone else who's of the same opinion. That they're "living in sin", I mean.'

'How so?'

'Some idiot is pestering them with anonymous letters and is clearly trying to split them up. Liljan has gotten several letters full of terrible slander against Gran, and Gran has received a similar note, the only difference being that it's about Liljan.'

'Who in the world would want to do something like that?'

'That's what they'd both like to find out, since that sort of thing gets pretty old in the long run. The last letter to Gran even threatened to turn them in to the police for immorality. Have you ever heard of such a thing – *turning them in for immorality!*'

'It might be a prank. If so, it's a definite sign of decline in the Norwegian sense of humor. Or maybe Bjørn Werner wrote the letters. It could be some kind of aftereffect from his religious studies.'

'I think one of Liljan's ex-boyfriends is behind it. She was with a couple of really twisted guys before she started going out with Gran.'

'Huh?' I was shocked. 'You mean to tell me that girl has already had lovers? How long has it been since her confirmation, anyway?'

'Liljan is twenty-two,' Sonja explained with a knowing expression. 'But you really are cute when you're morally shocked, Bernhard. I think you'll get that breakfast kiss after all . . .'

'I'm going to take a walk into town,' I said, grabbing my wide-brimmed Borsalino writer's hat. 'The weather's lovely, and I need to get my blood moving. I promise to come home afterwards and write like crazy.'

I turned around in the doorway.

'By the way, has Werner given any signs of life? He's been staying up at the haunted cabin for almost three weeks now.'

'No, at least Liljan hasn't heard anything from him. He'll be staying up there for over a month, you know. He's so excited about living the cabin life.'

'He certainly is, God help him! I'll see you later.'

There's no city as lovely as Oslo in the autumn. The Riviera in winter, sure, Paris in summer, all right, but *Oslo* in the autumn! When the air smells like a fine vintage champagne and the sunshine drapes over all the gray houses like a loving veil. Winter and decay are at the door; transience is already singing its dark psalm in the falling leaves, but for that very reason nature collects her last stores of warmth, her last colossal reserve of tenderness. In autumn our city is like a beautiful woman of thirty-eight.

I walked through Studenterlund towards the Theater Café, whistling as I went. I was in an excellent mood, even though I'd been struggling for three weeks with the material Gran had given me, the legend of Tore Gruvik; I hadn't managed to make anything out of it. The outlines I'd done for a thriller in the ghost story mode had turned out to be utter rubbish. You know the story about the cunning villain who takes advantage of the old legend, dressing up as a ghost to try to frighten off some heir so that he can buy the haunted house cheap and dig up the old Monte Cristo treasure hidden in the cellar? I had thought of doing something along those lines but realized in time that the idea had already been used about five thousand times before – by every crime writer from Conan Doyle to whoever writes the 'Story of the Day' in the Oslo evening paper. Yes, I was washed up, as dry as the Asian deserts where the old kingdoms of culture once flourished. There was nothing left to do but go down and register at the unemployment office. Sic transit gloria Bernhard Borgi. Tiddle-dee-dee, what lovely weather!

I went through the revolving doors and entered the restaurant. I spotted Kai Bugge sitting at one of the tables. He was about to pay the waiter, and as he was doing so I saw a piece of paper slip out of his wallet and fall to the floor without his noticing.

'Hello, old man,' I said, sitting down at his table.

'Hello.' He got up. 'Wait here a moment, I just have to make a phone call.'

While he was away, I picked up the paper from the floor and examined it. It was covered on both sides in a thin, distinctly nervous handwriting and proved to contain a summary of two dreams; obviously it had to do with one of Bugge's patients. When it comes to other people's private papers, I'm just as curious as any modern literary researcher, so I immediately set out to decipher the handwriting. It read as follows:

Dream. Night of August 9.

I dream that I'm floating in a lake, naked; my body gleams white and pure in the moonlight. I feel myself drifting slowly towards the bank, under a tall tree, a spruce tree, and just when the tree's shadow falls on me, it feels as though my body begins to wither in some strange way. My hands and feet take on a darker color and little by little turn completely black; they sort of go cold, then it spreads up my arms, up my legs and thighs, and finally over my whole body. I have the horrible feeling I've become leprous. Then suddenly I catch sight of a creature up on the bank, a large, shaggy beast standing there motionless, staring at me with a terribly intense, burning gaze. Only those eyes, that living, dreadful gaze, tells me that it's a *creature* and not just a shadow, part of the night's darkness. I feel an indescribable fear, but at the same time I'm strangely drawn towards the thing standing up there looking at me. I'm completely hypnotized; I can't move a muscle. Then suddenly the beast leaps from the shore, straight down towards me. It grabs

me and pulls me down into the depths. I can't breathe, my
lungs fill with water, I start to sink, sink . . .

Dream. Night of August 10.

I dream I'm running down an endlessly long road; I'm
fleeing something that's following me. I don't know what it
is, but the whole time I feel that it *is* there, just behind me.
I seem to feel its breath on the back of my neck, a warm,
repulsive breath. I don't dare turn around but just keep running – faster and faster, more and more frantic – until my
heart is about to burst. Then all at once I see I've arrived at a
train station; a train is just about to depart. A man is standing on the steps, waving to me; he wants to help me up into
the carriage. I can't see who he is; his features are hazy and
blurred, but nonetheless I have the feeling I know him. At
the last moment he pulls me in, and I fall exhausted to the
ground the very second the train sets off. I feel my pursuer
grasping for me, snatching at my clothes, but he doesn't get
me – I'm saved. Strangely enough it's only *now* that the fear
really sets in, now that I'm alone on the train with my res-
cuer. I wake up screaming, in a cold sweat of terror.

At the bottom of the page were these words in Bugge's
firm, easily recognizable handwriting:
Idea for 'large, shaggy beast': a bear.
Bugge had come back and caught me red-handed.
'Damn it,' he said, tearing the paper away from me,
'don't you have any tact?'
'You're obviously a little too careless to be entirely
trustworthy as a psychiatrist,' I remarked ironically. 'Or
maybe you psychoanalysts are in the habit of strewing
your patients' most intimate confidences around like leaf-
lets? Who wrote this, by the way? The author hasn't signed
their manuscript.'

'Sorry,' said Bugge, 'but you mustn't mistake a psychiatrist for a newspaper reporter. There's something called doctor-patient confidentiality.'

'Is there any reason to keep something like that secret? After all, I've already read what's on the paper, and it's only some silly and totally meaningless dreams. What makes someone have dreams like that, anyway? Maybe it's the new bread?'*

Bugge gave me an amiable smile.

'Everyone has those kinds of nightmares once in a while, don't they? That sort of nonsense doesn't mean anything, right?'

'That sort of nonsense is about the only thing that has any meaning at all,' said Bugge, gently correcting me. 'Dreams give a perspective into the psyche, the part below the surface – a deeper perspective than any other type of human expression can give us.'

'But what the hell do *these* dreams mean? What can you really get out of them? And what did you mean by the "idea" you jotted down on the paper underneath one of the dreams?'

Bugge had sat down and waved to a waiter. After three waiters had totally ignored us, passing us by like a high priest passes the beggars at the temple gates, we finally managed to order two glasses of light beer and a couple of sandwiches from the fourth.

'Since you've seen the paper anyway,' Bugge began, 'I guess there's no harm in telling you a little more. I can't disclose the patient's name, but I can tell you in confidence that this analysis I'm working on now is the most interesting case I've seen in my ten years of practice.'

He took a large gulp of the beer, which he seemed to find very tasty.

'If you were a man with even an average education, you would surely know what happens in this sort of analysis;

after all, the market is teeming with popular science books that illustrate our methods in a simple, easy to understand way. You would know that interpretation of dreams plays an essential role in the analysis, and that, among other things, that interpretation consists in examining what impression the patient has of the dream's various elements.

'In many cases these impressions or associations can reveal what thoughts are hidden behind the dream's flickering stream of images, and by following just one of these associations to where it leads, we can often get down to whole hidden complexes of ideas, down to the so-called *repressed* ideation.'

He fell silent for a moment and looked searchingly into his beer glass.

'Go on,' I said. 'I don't understand a word of this, so you may as well keep going.'

'Sooner or later in an analysis we usually come to a turning point, a situation where the patient will make every effort to *conceal* as much as possible from the analyst. Their dreams will get more and more distorted and impossible to interpret, and the patient will lack any insight into the dreams. This is the critical stage of the analysis, the moment when the analyst has finally reached the secret closed door, and all that's needed is an "open sesame" to make the cave wall slide open. Every patient is the keeper of his own illness, and he defends his neurosis with a desperate energy; after all, that illness has become his way of life, his *style*, you might say, and it often takes months or years before the analyst is able to break through his defenses. These dreams you've just read illustrate one of these critical situations. These dreams provide the key to a closed door in the patient's mind; that's why they were only able to give a single insight into one dream and nothing at all for the other.'

Bugge delivered his lecture in a smooth, fluent tone of

voice. These sorts of explanations usually bore me, but Bugge has his own compelling way of talking when discussing such things, and for some strange reason I had the feeling that all of this somehow concerned me. I leaned forward.

'If I understand you right,' I said, 'this "crisis" occurs in every psychoanalysis. So what's so remarkable about this case you're working on now?'

Bugge knocked the ash from his cigarette with a meaningful gesture.

'The reason this case is so interesting is that I've stumbled on a kind of dream I've never dealt with before in my practice. I admit my discovery isn't entirely new; this sort of dream has been discussed in the psychological literature before, but only superficially. There has been great doubt as to whether this type of dream even really exists; some have conjectured that it's merely a matter of so-called "coincidence". But if such dreams really do exist, it will open whole new perspectives into the study of the mind – '

'What sort of dream are you talking about, anyway?'

'I'm still not entirely sure; my hypothesis is mostly based on a hunch, so I'm not ready to discuss it yet. Wait – and read my next book.'

'The hell with your next book,' I said peevishly and got up. 'Incidentally, I have to go home now and work on *my* next book. It's looming over me like a nightmare. Have you ever dreamt you had an elephant sitting on top of you? That's a new type of dream *I've* discovered lately. So long.'

I sauntered homewards and let the cool, mild autumn air flow through my lungs. But my spirits had sunk several degrees. Why did Bugge always have to go around acting like the Sphinx of Giza? Why was he always trying to stir up people's curiosity? It was silly for me to get annoyed about it. What did some crazy patient of Bugge's have to do with me? I probably didn't even know the person in question; Bugge treated as many as ten to fifteen patients at a time. The whole business was totally irrelevant to me. But still . . . Why had I suddenly taken such a strange interest in this particular case?

The moment I opened the front door, Sonja came to meet me. Her face was strikingly pale, and there was an excited look in her eyes.

'Can you guess what's happened?' Her voice was hoarse with emotion.

'No. You look terrified. Did you put arsenic in the kids' porridge instead of cream of wheat?'

'Don't talk nonsense. Look at this article.'

She handed me the afternoon edition of the newspaper. My glance fell at once on what was undeniably a fairly sensational notice:

> *Young Oslo Man Vanishes in Østerdalen.*
> *A Peculiar Suicide.*

Bjørn Werner, a young Oslo man who has lately been living in a cabin in Svartskogen, a wooded area in Østerdalen, has been reported missing. Werner has been staying at the cabin alone for three weeks and is not known to have been in contact with anyone during that period. In his report to the Oslo police, the district sheriff claims to have definite evidence of suicide; footprints indicate that Werner must have drowned himself in Blue Lake, a small body of water near the cabin. All efforts to find the body, however, have proven fruitless due to the lake's great depth.

I had read enough and set the paper aside.

'My God,' I muttered. 'I can't believe it. Werner didn't have any reason to . . .'

'Don't you remember the story Gran told at our party? About Tore Gruvik – '

'But there can't possibly be anything to such a fantastic story. Things like that don't happen in real life and hardly even in books. I don't understand . . . No, it must be a mistake. He must have gotten lost in the woods or something.'

Just then the telephone rang. I answered it.

'Hello.' It was Gran's voice. 'Have you seen the paper?'

'I had it in my hand just now. What in the world does it all mean?'

'Well, it's hard to say. It looks like the story I told has taken on a certain relevance.'

'Do you know whether Werner had any reason to take his own life?'

'Absolutely not. He didn't have a care in the world. Just between you and me, I have a little theory about this business.'

'Spit it out.'

'I think there's been foul play. A murder, plain and simple.'

'But surely Werner didn't have any enemies?'

'We'll come back to that later. First listen to what I propose. I've just talked with Liljan and obviously she's really shaken up by all this, and what's more, she's dead set on going up to the cabin at once.'

'What for?'

'To shed some light on what really happened. But I don't want her going alone. So I suggest we organize a little expedition, all of us who were together at your place that evening – that is, minus some of the women. I've already spoken to Mørk and Bugge and they're both on board. I imagine you'll be wanting to come too. After all, it's the research trip I suggested you take three weeks ago – now you've actually got something for your new novel!'

'It sounds quite exciting, but what can we really accomplish with that sort of "expedition"? If Werner drowned in the lake and searching for his body is futile, then we don't stand much chance of finding him either. And if he was murdered, as you say, then it doesn't seem too likely that the possible murderer is still lurking around the scene of the crime.'

'As I said, it's Liljan who's dead set on going, and I'm pretty keen to investigate this case a little closer myself. I think there's something fishy going on, and I'd like to get to the bottom of it. You know that deep down I'm a detective at heart.'

'Do you know the way there?'

'Yes. I've been there once before – I went with Werner when he bought the cabin. Bring some clothes and food and come as soon as you can. The train leaves in an hour.'

I turned to Sonja, who had stood beside me listening to the conversation.

'What do you suggest?'

'We go,' said Sonja. Her cheeks had grown flushed and her voice was excited.

'You too? And the kids?'

'Can stay with my mother for a while. I've wanted to see that cabin and lake ever since Gran told his story that night.'

I nodded. I had felt the little flame of curiosity burning in me too.

'All right,' I said into the receiver. 'We'll meet at the station in forty-five minutes.'

CHAPTER THREE

In which a strange expedition sets off into the wilderness

IT WAS SOMETHING OF AN IMPROVISED HOLIDAY we set out on, the six of us sitting together in the train compartment a couple of hours later. Bugge, Mørk, and Gran had managed to get off work on an hour's notice; Sonja had given the theater the excuse of a serious family illness, and with a tired sigh I had laid my dreadnought of a novel back on the shelf. Liljan was the only one of us who was totally free of commitments, a person who spent most of her time at nightclubs and thus could take a trip like this with a clear conscience, but then she was also the one who'd had this rather baroque whim. Kind of funny, I told myself, for six modern, enlightened people – representatives of a civilization of steel and concrete – to suddenly set off into the wilderness to investigate an old ghost story. But Werner's strange death was reason enough.

As might be expected, the news of her brother's disappearance had made Liljan nervous and upset, so naturally she was the center of attention.

'Were you very fond of your brother?' Gran said, leaning towards her in a way that could not be misunderstood.

'Yes, I was very fond of him. There's always been a kind of strange bond between us. It's like we didn't need to talk in order for each of us to know what the other was thinking.'

Liljan lit a cigarette. I noticed that her right hand was shaking.

'I remember something that happened several years

ago. Bjørn was living by himself in a little apartment on Drammensvei – back then he lived like a total recluse and didn't see other people. If I remember right, he was busy with his thesis on Dante. One day he had gone out dressed too lightly for the winter cold and caught a bad case of pneumonia. It hadn't occurred to him to call the doctor as soon as possible – besides, he didn't have a phone – he just went to bed and hoped it would pass. That very day I suddenly got the feeling there was something wrong with Bjørn, a totally inexplicable suspicion that he was in danger. I went to his apartment right away and found him lying on the floor with a terrible fever. I had him brought to a hospital, where he was saved in the nick of time . . .'

She took a long, deep drag from her cigarette. Her pretty, slightly nearsighted eyes had taken on an almost feverish glow.

'The odd thing is that for the past few days I've had a similar feeling. I warned Bjørn three weeks ago not to take the trip – not because of that ridiculous old ghost story, but for a totally different reason – I don't even know why myself. The whole time he's been away I've had this oppressive feeling that he's in danger, that he's being threatened by something terrible. Can you imagine where a feeling like that might come from?'

A stream of landscapes flowed by outside the window; we sat in silence, staring out at the endless telegraph wires running up and down, up and down, with something of the drab monotony of everyday life. There's not much to see through a window like that one: here and there a cow, obviously an adherent of the materialistic school of thought, walking around a clover meadow with an irritating expression of well-being, or else some rural-looking person loitering around a train station with his whole forearm stuck in his pocket. Aside from a hike in Jotunheimen or a lecture on oceanography, a train journey like that one is the most boring thing I can think of. Finally I began to find the silence oppressive.

'I'd like to ask all of you something,' I said. 'Why did you suddenly say to hell with your jobs and daily routines and set out on such a strange expedition into the unknown? What do you hope to achieve?'

'I've already answered that question,' Gran declared. 'As I've said, I think it's a case of foul play – my old detective's instincts tell me so. I'm expecting it to be a most interesting assignment.'

'And you, Bugge?'

'Well,' Bugge shrugged his shoulders, 'I'm interested in this case for a number of reasons. First of all, I'd like to find the psychological basis for Werner's suicide – for the moment I'm working under the assumption that it is in fact a suicide. Secondly, I'm eager to take a closer look at that old legend about Tore Gruvik, especially the suicidal mania supposedly connected with the spot. By staying there myself I can – as Gran put it – study the effect on my own body.'

I felt a strong aversion to the whole business when Bugge repeated that expression. What was really the point of such an experiment? To be honest, what I wanted most of all was to get off at the next station and take the first train back to Oslo. But I couldn't do that. Once you're on a slippery slope, there's nothing you can do but keep sliding down.

'I imagine there's a psychological connection between that old legend and Werner's disappearance,' Bugge went on. 'I think some important law has been at work in this case, and I intend to find out what it is. I suffer from the researcher's gold fever, the eternal hunger to find a pattern in the chaos, a meaning in the meaningless. I'm a slave to science.'

'Now it's your turn, Mørk,' I said. 'What's *your* real agenda for this trip?'

'In the first place, Werner was my friend,' said Mørk. 'I'm interested in his fate; he was a seeker, after all. Secondly, I see this case in a totally different light from the rest of you. I don't think that what happened is something as banal as a crime, a murder – you've been reading too much Nick Carter, my dear Gran – nor do I think it's an ordinary case of suicide. To put it simply, I believe we're dealing with an occult phenomenon, an encounter with the supernatural.'

Mørk folded his hands over his stomach and looked intently at Bugge as he went on talking.

'That's why I'm interested in undertaking this "expedition" with all of you, with five people blinded by modern materialism, totally unaware that there's a world beyond the one we can see and touch. I'd like to see, for example, you, Bugge, faced with a hole in your unimaginative worldview, with a great paradox for which your endless formulas and schemas can't find any explanation. I'd like to see so-called common sense knock its head against the wall; I'd like to see so-called science admit its total lack of insight into nature's secrets. In short, I'd like to see an entire way of looking at the world exposed as totally bankrupt. We've lived far too long on crumbs from the nineteenth century's table . . .'

Mørk spoke in a relatively low, yet intense tone of voice. Again I felt the same chilling sensation of aversion; damn Gran for bringing me along! I cast a longing glance through the window; for once the sight of the cows in the clover meadow and the farmer with his hands in his pockets seemed cheering.

It struck me right away that there was something dreary and cramped about the little woodland hamlet where we got off the train. A cluster of small, ugly houses was grouped around a slightly larger hovel that was clearly the town's station building. It was late in the evening and life in the village appeared totally extinct; there wasn't a soul to be seen. All the lights were out in the houses, and the windowpanes stared out into the moonlight like blind, black eyes. The place lay nestled in a sort of hollow in the terrain. Tree-covered hills rose on all sides, the dark ridges standing out with knife-sharp contours against the violet evening sky. There was evidently a little river close by; the flow of the running water was the only sound to be heard in the silence. But it wasn't the gentle, pleasant rippling sound that such creeks usually make. It was a harsh tone, an ugly, lingering dissonance.

'The underworld must be something like this,' I whispered jokingly to Sonja. 'Isn't that the river Lethe we hear in the background?'

Gran found the road and we started our climb. It was a typical winding, bumpy Norwegian country road with a fairly steep slope, not exactly inviting if you're driving a luxury car, but manageable for a modern tank. A moonlit stroll along a romantic old road like that one might have its charm, if the landscape looked like something out of a poem by Heine. But that hike was anything but charming. I've never seen a denser forest than that one. The trees formed a kind of wall on both sides of the road; it was like moving through the bottom of a narrow ravine. The moon cast a milky light over the road ahead of us and the nearest tree trunks. Further into the thicket it was impossible to distinguish a single tree; your eyes encountered only a wall of darkness. The whole time we heard the rasping of the river, which ran almost parallel to the road. I knew what that hoarse, obnoxious sound reminded me of: it was like *laughter*, a croaking, malevolent mirth.

'You can't really accuse this place of having much natural beauty,' Bugge remarked drily. He was walking beside me with his hands in his pockets. 'The people up here can't make a living off selling postcards to tourists, anyway.'

'This place really is horrible,' Sonja whispered with delight, pressing herself against my arm tightly. '*Svartskogen* – the black forest – the name is certainly fitting.'

'Can you imagine Werner wanting to live in such a creepy place?' I murmured. 'I can certainly see how that eerie old legend got started here. What kind of people live in these parts anyway? You must have seen them, Gran?'

Gran laughed. 'They're almost as weird as their surroundings,' he said. 'Shy and reserved and quite difficult to communicate with. People are often rather odd in these small, isolated communities.'

'There's something frightening about all of nature,' Mørk said. 'Humans once lived in harmony with nature, and nature was divine then, but after man's fall it became demonic. "Deserted altars are a dwelling place for demons," says Ernst Jünger. Pan is a fallen god, and those who go out into nature to find him, find only a demonic being. Thus the modern gospel of nature is also a demonic gospel.'

'Nice job saying the word "demonic" so many times in the same breath,' said Bugge.

'A puerile remark,' said Mørk.

We had been walking at a leisurely pace and chatting for maybe half an hour when Sonja suddenly grabbed my arm hard.

'Isn't that someone coming up the road over there?' she exclaimed. 'I think I hear footsteps.'

We stopped for a moment and could clearly hear the sound of steps coming closer. And a few seconds later a tall figure came into view around the next bend in the road, apparently a man. He was walking straight towards us; the hard, metallic moonlight gave a slightly unreal, almost luminescent cast to his features. I stepped back instinctively to fall a little behind the others.

'Ghost number one,' Gran declared stoically. 'Stay calm, ladies and gentlemen.'

The figure stopped abruptly several yards in front of us, suddenly standing stock-still, staring at us.

'You folks out for a picnic?' asked a voice with an unmistakable Oslo accent.

'Why, it's Bråten!' cried Gran. 'Hello, old friend. We thought you were a ghost.'

The two men shook hands warmly. Gran turned towards the rest of us.

'This is my old school friend, Einar Bråten,' he explained. 'He failed his civil service exam so badly that he wound up as a sheriff here in the jungle – they didn't have any use for him in civilization. Let's have a little chat with him; he probably hasn't talked with any civilized people since the last time I was up here and visited him.'

After the usual introductions, Bråten accompanied us. He seemed like an intelligent and friendly person and spoke with a warm, manly voice.

'What brings you here?' he asked. Gran explained the situation to him.

'Weren't you the one who made the report to the Oslo police? About Werner's suicide?'

'Yes, it was me. I don't think there's any doubt Werner drowned himself in Blue Lake. The tracks make it quite clear.'

'How so?'

'On the morning of August 17 I found Werner's hat and shotgun lying by the shore of the lake. Beside them was the body of his dog, shot in the head with a shotgun blast. I found fresh footprints in the soft soil and investigated them at once. They went *to* the shore, but they didn't come back. What's more, the last footprint clearly shows he must have taken the plunge and thrown himself in.'

'In deep water?'

'Yes. From a fairly low plateau, about a yard above the water's surface. Later I examined the tracks more thoroughly and determined they were made by Werner's shoes, a pair of large, sturdy athletic shoes, flat in front and with unusually wide soles; I had seen him wearing them when I met him on his way up a couple of weeks earlier. What's more, Werner's name was on the dog's collar; the fact that the dog was shot also points to suicide. People often kill a favorite pet – their dog, for example – before they commit suicide; then in a way they have a traveling companion in death. I've come across several such cases in my experience.'

'Didn't you search the cabin?'

'Yes, of course. It was empty and had clearly been abandoned during the night; a paraffin lamp that must have been lit the previous evening was still burning. Otherwise everything was in order there, no sign of a hasty departure, nor anything pointing to – how can I put it? – an attack of mental disturbance. Books and furniture were in their proper places; everything was as neat and tidy as a modern business office. It looks as though he had a leisurely dinner, then took his dog and rifle and strolled down to the lake. I figure it must have happened sometime around midnight.'

The rest of us walked in silence, listening to the conversation. The words flowed simply and naturally, like a chat over coffee, but all the same there was something improbable about it all, something dreamlike. I rubbed my eyes: was I awake?

'You've done your work thoroughly, my dear colleague,' said Gran, smiling. 'It's a shame that a man of your caliber should be stuck tramping around up here in this wasteland; you belong at Scotland Yard. But there is one thing I'd very much like to know. How is it that you discovered these footprints the very morning after Werner's – er – suicide? Surely you don't patrol this vast territory of yours every day? And by the way, what are you doing wandering around the woods all by yourself at this time of night?'

'That's another story,' said Bråten. 'I don't know whether you've noticed, but even in these parts something happens every now and then. If you've been keeping up with the news, you might remember the Haugestad murders?'

'That rings a bell – '

'Right. A man from here in the village killed his two brothers and was caught afterwards; it turned out that he was insane, stark raving mad. But somewhere in his disturbed mind there must have been a bit of sense, because he managed to escape and is still at large. We have reason to believe he's living here in the woods somewhere.'

'An insane killer here in the woods? That doesn't sound too pleasant. No doubt it's easy to hide in here?'

'Very easy. The area is full of caves. There are also a couple of old, abandoned shanties along the river; I went and checked them out this evening.'

'A bit risky, wasn't it?'

Bråten patted his jacket pocket.

'I'm ready for just about anything. It's because of this manhunt that I came across Werner's footprints. I had talked with him briefly when he was on his way up here, and I warned him against staying in the cabin alone with this crazy killer on the loose. He ignored the warning, but on the morning of August 16 – the day of his suicide – I got a message from him in which he claimed to have discovered the fugitive's hiding place. He asked me to come and see him the following morning, he wanted to talk to me. I complied with his request and went up to the cabin on the 17th, but Werner had disappeared.'

'In other words, he had given you a *written* message?'

'Yes, oddly enough. He had left a visiting card in my mailbox while I was out. If speaking with me were so important, it's strange he would make the long trek to the village and then not wait an hour for me to get back. If he had done that, he might still be alive today.'

'So no one opened the door when he went to your house? Do you know whether anyone in the village even saw him that morning?'

'I don't. Why do you ask?'

'Well, it's possible that . . . anyway, we'll see.'

The road became even more winding and arduous as we went on. The moon had temporarily taken refuge behind a cloud, so the landscape was now shrouded in an almost Egyptian darkness. It had gotten considerably harder to see in front of ourselves; I stumbled a couple of times over tree roots slung across the road like long serpents. As I walked I thought about what the sheriff had told us about the crazed murderer, a restless, desperate creature hiding somewhere in the woods. It was strange how well that fit with the mood of the place. There was something like it in the air; I had felt it the moment we stepped off the train at the station. It certainly was a pleasant holiday I had ahead of me!

Fear of the dark has been one of my few great weaknesses ever since childhood. Now as I walked I peered into the black thicket, where the spreading branches constantly formed new shapes, Medusa heads that suddenly sprang out of the darkness, grinned at me and then disappeared again. Every now and then I thought I glimpsed a human face in there too, with pale, contorted features, the face of a criminal . . .

If I hear any more edifying descriptions of this place and its tourist attractions, I told myself, I'm going back to Oslo, no matter if I have to make my way there on a handcar. Even if my wife asks for a divorce, and even if I have to listen to Bugge's malicious laughter the rest of my life. I'd had enough.

'And what do you think, Bråten? Do you have a theory about Werner's suicide?' asked Gran.

'I couldn't say. I didn't even know him.'

'Then you don't believe in the old legend?'

'To tell the truth, no.' Bråten smiled. 'I'm a policeman. I don't believe in ghosts and goblins.'

We stopped. We had reached a clearing, a small open place in the forest. At the end of this clearing, nestled tightly under the trees, itself forming a part of the cold, whispering darkness of the woods, was Dead Man's Cabin.

CHAPTER FOUR

In which Bråten provides information

I WAS AMAZED when I saw how large the cabin was. I had expected something along the lines of an old worm-eaten shed, the usual miniature shanty, but in fact it was a small farmhouse. There was something massive and hulking about it, something almost majestic, as it rose up among the trees. The cracked gray walls were over-grown with a layer of moss and lichen; it was reminiscent of an old troll that had been turned to stone. I couldn't help thinking of Gran's expression: that it had become a 'Sleeping Beauty's castle in the popular imagination'. That must be how fairy tales originate: a man roams around the woods alone at night and suddenly stops before a house like this one. He stands as though spellbound, staring at it for several minutes, maybe hours; then the myth takes shape in his mind, the myth of the enchanted castle.

Sonja stood beside me, apparently thinking the same thing.

'The witch's house in the tale of Hansel and Gretel must have looked something like this,' she said. 'But I don't see any cakes in the windows.'

'I'm more interested in the tale of Bernhard and Sonja,' I said. 'Shall we go inside?'

We went in. The interior contrasted sharply with the exterior; once we had lit the paraffin lamps it proved to be downright cozy. The house showed signs of having been renovated fairly recently; the ceiling and walls were cov-ered in fragrant new planks painted in light and carefree colors. The spacious living room was equipped with various pieces of furniture you wouldn't normally find in a cabin: a birch veneer desk, a couple of deep, comfortable leather chairs, and several shelves of books. Besides the living room the house had three smaller rooms with two bunks in each, an old-fashioned but neat and tidy little kitchen, a very low-ceilinged attic, and a tiny cellar. Outside a kind of veranda faced the clearing.

I had expected something totally different, something frankly awful, and so needless to say I was pleasantly surprised; this could pass for a respectable country house. Maybe this 'holiday' wasn't such a crazy idea after all?

We put down our luggage, and after a fairly cursory glance over the premises we began to make ourselves comfortable in the living room.

'It's really nice here,' I said after settling down – as was my habit – in the best chair. 'Werner had good taste. And so this is supposed to be the devil's stomping ground?'

Gran started to fiddle with his rucksack and a moment later pulled out an impressive bottle of aquavit, newly acquired from some infamous bootlegger at an appalling price. Sonja, who only needs to smell a kitchen at a distance of a hundred yards to be taken over by the spirit of domesticity, immediately went to get glasses from the cupboard.

'Sit down and have a drink with us,' Gran said to Bråten. 'I'm sure you have other interesting things to tell.'

The glasses were set on the table and each was filled in turn with the splendid golden liquid. We sat smacking our lips for a while after the first sip; it was like oasis water to a desert nomad, like cool rainfall after a drought.

Bugge was the first to stop smacking. 'I'd love to hear a little more about this Tore Gruvik,' he said. 'I can't stop thinking about that old legend. You were Gran's source, right, Bråten? He heard the story from you?'

'Of course.' Bråten gave an ironic smile. He obviously found the whole subject a little childish. 'I'll be happy to tell you all I know.'

'There were a couple of unclear points in the story as Gran told it,' said Bugge. 'How can we know for certain that Gruvik actually committed that double murder? And how do we know he went mad afterwards and jumped into Blue Lake? If I understand correctly, there were no eyewitnesses to the drama and the bodies were never found.'

'There's a very simple explanation.' Bråten's face had once again taken on the expression of an expert. 'Gruvik left behind a diary containing a confession of the crime and a declaration that he intended to commit suicide. That is, it wasn't actually a confession in so many words; it was only a few fragments and incoherent sentences, mostly unreadable gibberish showing the man had completely lost his mind. We still keep the diary in our archives as an old relic from the case – you can see it if you like. As for eyewitnesses –'

'Were there eyewitnesses after all?'

'No, not to the murder; we have only Gruvik's own vague words as to that. But as for his suicide, there were – if not *eye*witnesses – what you might call *ear*witnesses. On the night of August 22, 1831, there happened to be some loggers here in the woods near Blue Lake. All of a sudden they heard sharp, piercing screams coming from the lake, like those of someone in great danger. They ran in the direction of the sound, but when they got to the water there was nothing to be seen. Later, however, they found footprints indicating a man had jumped in – probably something like those footprints of Werner's that I found.'

'In other words, Gruvik *screamed* just before he drowned himself?'

'Apparently. After all, it's not so unusual for madmen to scream.'

It was funny seeing Bugge so caught up in all of this. He's usually the very picture of seriousness, a man who lives in the moment and focuses on the task at hand, and now here he was discussing an ancient, half-forgotten legend with the same interest an Egyptologist shows for a newly discovered royal tomb.

'Since you're so captivated by this old mystery,' Bråten continued, 'I can tell you a couple of details I probably didn't mention to Gran before. It has to do with the ghost story, which is still quite a sensation in these parts. You already know the legend about how Blue Lake *pulls* people to it?'

'I do.'

'And you've heard that Gruvik is said to return in his own peculiar way? That no one has ever seen his ghost?'

'Yes, thanks, I'm up to speed.'

'Well, then. The story requires a little addendum. He's been *heard*. You remember I mentioned that Tore Gruvik took his own life the night of August 22, 1831 – almost exactly 110 years ago. Every year on the night of August 22, you can supposedly hear Gruvik's death cry coming from the lake; several so-called reliable people down in the village claim to have heard it.'

'You haven't heard it yourself, in other words?' Gran interjected.

'Of course not. It's all just nonsense, the product of frightened farmers' imaginations. I grew up in a place with electricity, after all. Besides, I've never been here in the area at that exact time of year.'

'The night of August 22?' I mumbled. 'It's the night of the 19th now. So we still have three days of fun ahead of us.'

Bråten took another sip from his glass and set it down again. His hand slid caressingly down the stem.

'There is one other thing that's a little strange,' he con-

tinued, 'one more funny little detail that shows how back-
ward the people are up here. The late Tore Gruvik had lost
his left foot in an accident; he walked with a wooden leg.
Now "trustworthy" people still claim to this day to have
seen footprints in the woods from a man with an artificial
left leg; in other words, the tracks of Gruvik himself, the
restless spirit, the lost soul. As for me, I've never heard of
lost souls leaving behind footprints . . .'

I no longer found listening to all of this so unpleasant.
The glass of spirits I had drunk was burning inside me with
a calm, pleasant little flame; I was enjoying myself. I leaned
all the way back in the chair and curled my toes with contentment. I've always been relentlessly consistent in oppos-
ing Friedrich Nietzsche's motto, 'Live dangerously!', with
Bernhard Borge's words: 'Live comfortably!'

Bråten looked at Bugge with a smile.

'And now I hope what I've told you hasn't frightened you
too much?'

'On the contrary,' said Bugge. 'I almost think I'm ready
to fall in love with this place.'

'Understandable,' snickered Mørk. 'Very easily understandable. Let's summarize: A lake that sucks people into it,
an invisible phantom that screams and leaves footprints, a
crazed double murderer on the loose, wandering around
desperately in the dark of night. You might indeed say this
is a fitting atmosphere for a psychoanalyst.'

Bråten looked at his watch.

'Good lord,' he said. 'It's already half past midnight. I
have to get back before sunrise. Thanks for your hospitality.'

He got up and walked to the door. At the threshold he
turned around.

'It's probably best if you keep an eye out for our
madman. If he should turn up around here, try to placate
him and keep him here till you get hold of me. I don't really

think he's as dangerous as I might have made him sound. But there's no harm in a little caution . . .'

We went to bed fifteen minutes later. Several of us were tired after the long trip; the alcohol had done its part too, and in short it felt great to hit the sack. We divided up the available rooms in a more or less rational way: Sonja and I claimed the one adjoining the kitchen, Liljan took the one next door, and Bugge and Gran shared the third small bedroom. Mørk slept alone in the living room. I thought it was a little surprising that Liljan and Gran didn't sleep together, but that sort of thing is supposed to be reserved for married couples, and it's awkward when there are other people around. It could also be that they had been following the discussion in the newspaper about young people and camping trips and had taken to heart what the 'conscientious mother who was once young herself' has to say on the subject. Enough about that; in any case Liljan slept alone.

Sonja was already lying down when I climbed into my bunk. I lay on my back for a while, staring at the ceiling, where a moth was making a series of vain attempts to punch a hole and get out into the open air.

'Listen,' I said. 'There's something I've been thinking about for the past six hours. I still don't really understand what we're doing up here.'

Some odd little sounds came from Sonja. It sounded like laughter.

'There isn't much you really do understand, is there, Bernhard?'

'I beg your pardon? Don't be catty, little wife. You should be grateful to have a husband as intelligent as me.'

'Are you sure about that?'

'Absolutely. Let me remind you that I took an IQ test last year and scored a mental age of thirteen, which is pretty good, considering one of our leading professors turned out to have a mental age of eight.'

'I'm proud of you, Bernhard.'

'Oh, darling, it's nothing . . .'

'Good night, then, sweet little hubby.'

'Hm. Good night.'

It was gorgeous August weather when I woke up the next morning; the mild, friendly autumn sun streamed like a white river through the dew-bright air and flowed into a little pool of light on the floor. That, combined with an unmistakable waft of coffee from the kitchen beside me, put me in a lyrical morning mood. As I got dressed, I sang one of the arias from *Rigoletto* to my wife through the wall into the kitchen, where she was toiling away at the stove with the zealous diligence of a slave.

I was completely free of the previous night's spooky mood when I went in to the covered breakfast table in the living room. I hardly remembered what we had talked about and had entirely forgotten my own macabre reflections. Bugge was sitting over by the fire, immersed in a hardcover journal. His face had a totally absent expression; he looked like he was concentrating on a problem.

'Good morning,' I said. 'What have you got there?'

He looked up from the book.

'I've taken the liberty of conducting a little raid on the papers Bjørn Werner left behind,' he said. 'And I've found an exceedingly interesting document, a *document humain*, as Zola would have called it.'

'You pique my curiosity. What kind of document do you mean?'

'A diary.'

'An ordinary diary?'

'No, an extremely unusual one. A strange little text that illustrates in a deeply realistic way a man's spiritual crisis, his plunge into great madness.'

'Aha, perhaps it's a copy of the book Bråten was talking about yesterday? The confession Tore Gruvik left behind.'

'Funny you should guess that. No, this one is quite a bit more recent in date. In fact, it's Bjørn Werner's personal diary. Would you care to read it?'

'You bet I would.'

I took the book and looked at it; I recognized Werner's stiff, regular handwriting on the cover right away. The book contained about one hundred closely written pages.

'This is a whole novel. Where should I start?'

'You can start with the entry for August 1. There aren't very many pages, but you should read them carefully. I imagine they hold the key to what we might give the slightly melodramatic title of "The Mystery of the Blue Lake".'

CHAPTER FIVE

In which a madman's diary is presented

I'M PRESENTING Bjørn Werner's diary to my readers here, but not as a psychopathic curiosity meant to excite a thrill-seeking audience. Nor do I have any interest in exposing my late friend's idiosyncrasies and eccentricities to the public. I am doing it solely because Bugge still insists that this document was the most important evidence in the case; without this diary it probably would have been impossible to clear everything up fully. I have to admit that, just like most of Bugge's other claims, this one is pretty much beyond me. I've read through this 'fragment of a magical life'* several times and pondered it seriously, and I've come to the conclusion that for the most part these pages consist of nothing but incoherent and meaningless fantasies, some of it pure delirium. I don't understand how something like that can mean anything at all. But you should never be too sure of your own judgment; therefore I'm turning this 'document' over to the public, so that readers, if they wish, can put their own psychological acumen to the test.

Bjørn Werner has the floor:

Aug. I. Went up to the cabin today. Pouring down the whole way. The rain flowed in dense, cold streams from the gray-blue sky, and Bella and I were both soaked when we arrived. I enjoy walking in the woods in that sort of weather; it's like suddenly being much closer to nature. The fresh, herbal smell of wet trees is delightful – it must be how the world smelled in the primordial age, the virgin earth!

The cabin is nice and watertight after the renovations, really a luxury cabin; it was a blessing to come inside and peel off my clothes. Strangely enough I think a number of things have been altered since I was here last; it seems to me that the furniture is arranged differently, and it even looks as though someone has messed with some of the fixtures recently. But no one could have been here while I was away. The door was locked and the windows latched, and there's no sign of a break-in. So it must just be my imagination.

Spent the first evening in the cozy company of my books. Read Flaubert's brilliant distillation of the ancient world, *The Temptation of St Anthony*.

Aug. 2. Went on a reconnaissance tour of the woods today and was sadly disappointed. I was told there would be a lot of grouse here at this time of year. But these woods seem totally extinct, devoid of all life. It's peculiar; I haven't even spotted a single songbird here – at the beginning of August! There's just *one* bird's voice I've constantly heard, sometimes far off, sometimes close by. I have the impression that it's always the same bird; it *screams*. It's probably a crow, although I've never heard a crow make that sort of noise before; it's a deeper and fiercer sound, like a wounded animal makes. I haven't seen it yet, however, even though I've been keeping an eye out. If I do spot it, I'll shoot it. It gets on my nerves.

Bella has been acting strangely today. Usually she's bursting with energy and the thrill of the hunt when I take her with me on these hikes. But this time she was unusually meek; she slunk almost disheartened at my side and showed remarkably little interest in everything. A couple of times I tried to get her to run ahead and sniff out the terrain a little, but she simply wouldn't. She clearly wanted to stay close by me – I don't know why. She must be ill, though I didn't notice anything wrong with her on the way here. When I get back to Oslo, I'll have her checked out by a vet.

Aug. 3. Rain again today, stayed inside most of the day. Took up Dante's *Divina Commedia* again, probably the only book in the world that deserves the adjective 'divine' in its title. Dante's journey is a brilliant allegory; it is *mankind's* journey through existence, through hell and purgatory to paradise, salvation:

> But before me stood *Beatrice*, the pure one,
>> turned towards the beast which in itself unites
>> with two natures one person alone.
> Standing there, her face enshrouded in a veil,
>> she surpassed her own beauty of olden times
>> far more than once she did every other female.*

Along the same lines, I also picked up Strindberg's *Inferno*. I refuse to believe that Strindberg was ever insane. The 'powers' he writes about do not seem the chimeras of a madman's brain; he experienced them while he was awake and lucid. When you read his fervent confession, you understand that such powers must exist – objectively! Somewhere there's someone toying with human beings, pulling invisible strings, playing with them like dolls in a puppet show.

What does it mean to be mad, anyway? Doesn't it mean having more delicate and sensitive nerves than other people, having developed totally new mental organs, mental antennae; in short, being able to see in a world where everyone else is blind? Perhaps the madman is a refraction phenomenon, the first rough draft of a new kind of person, a new species on Earth?

Aug. 4. Went on another walk in the woods today and was disappointed again. You would think a plague had wiped out the birds here. Where have they gone? At least one good thing came out of my hike: I got a glimpse of the crow, a large, black beast, one of the biggest and ugliest crows I've ever seen. It suddenly came fluttering out of the thicket and flew right over my head, shrieking the whole time with its hoarse, grating voice, its clumsy wings flapping in the wind, beating the air into foam beneath it. There was something strangely human about it, something both impotent and defiant, something hateful. I found it repulsive. When I was within ten yards of it, I raised my gun and fired off a salvo. I must have hit it; it took a spray of buckshot, but it didn't fall. It merely fluttered back into the woods again, casting mocking shrieks at me. Yes, it actually mocked me! But just you wait, my friend, I'll get hold of you yet. You pollute the air here in the woods. I've got another cartridge here with your name on it.

Bella behaved strangely again today, but she wasn't apathetic and disinterested like yesterday. She simply seemed *scared*. Several times she stopped with a jerk, suddenly standing stock-still on four stiff legs, sniffing the air with her long, narrow muzzle. Her eyes stared big and bright straight ahead of her; there was fear in them, an animal's instinctive fear. I had to tug her to make her keep walking; then she whimpered, she didn't want to go any further. I tried to follow the direction of her gaze, but there was nothing to see except the lake, which lay glistening bluish-green in the faint sunlight.

Aug. 5. Took a walk down to Blue Lake this morning, an odd little body of water. It's opaque and cloudy, of course, like all stagnant lakes, but it has an unusual color that invariably gives the impression of *depth*, an almost dizzying depth – it's like staring down into outer space.

Maybe there really is something magnetic about such lakes, something that draws you in. You have the feeling there are violent whirlpools somewhere deep, deep down beneath the motionless surface, waiting to suck you in. It's a bit like the feeling you get when standing safely behind a guardrail, looking down into a waterfall, peering down into the raging white torrents. You suddenly have the urge to swing over the rail, to catch yourself off guard, to act lightning-fast and impulsively, to get out in front of your consciousness's attempts to brake or control you, to make a single blissful, desperate leap into the horror . . .

Read *St Anthony* this afternoon. But I no longer feel much like reading; I keep having to put the book down and pace back and forth across the floor. Bella is lying over in the corner staring at me with her bright, attentive eyes. I don't know why, but I suddenly feel so uneasy and restless; it's like I've got some kind of itch in my blood.

Aug. 6. Feel calmer today. I must have been a little under the weather yesterday. Is it possible that weird old legend has made some kind of impression on me? As I lay reading this evening, I suddenly realized that I was no longer registering any of the letters on the page; I just lay there daydreaming, thinking about Tore Gruvik. But as soon as I became conscious of it, I immediately dismissed the thought. What was the expression Gran used when we were all together at Borge's? He mentioned something about how I was going to 'put my nerves of steel and concrete to the test'.

Nerves of steel and concrete? Right.

Aug. 7. I can't stand to read any more of Strindberg; his grotesque visions get on my nerves. It's a monster of a book, it'll tear me to pieces if I go on with it. There's something unhealthy about that kind of literature that ties our minds in knots without undoing them afterwards. Dante's *Commedia* is a book one can return to again and again. It's like a thunderstorm, but it has a thunderstorm's cleansing properties. It's like a wild, foaming river that runs out to a calm, clear sea; it flows in peace, harmony, and purity . . .

Aug. 8. A peculiar unease has come over me. It struck me at once when I came home from my morning hike today: *someone has been in here.* It was exactly the same feeling I had when I walked through the door the first day, but this time I'm totally sure. Something has been changed. I can't say exactly what, but I'm convinced that someone must have messed with my things, tampered with them. Was there really someone in here? The windows were latched and the door locked. When someone has just been in a room, you can usually sense a little warmth in the air, the warmth of blood, a hint of something alive. But a new *coldness* had suddenly come into this room, a strange atmosphere . . .

I stood spellbound for a couple of seconds, looking around at the different objects in the room. My attention was drawn to some small scratches on the table. I couldn't remember seeing them before; they looked like little claw marks. Then Bella started barking violently at the ceiling; her eyes were fixed on it, her tail whipping furiously against the floor.

I looked up. There was nothing to be seen in the room. So I took my gun under my arm and went out.

There on the chimney sat the crow. It was totally motionless, almost like a stuffed bird, staring at me. There was something dull, something *sooty*, about its black feathers, as though it had just come up through the chimney. It wasn't shrieking anymore. It just stared with a cold, piercing look; it had human eyes. I was seized with a bitter fury, brought my rifle up to my chin, and fired both barrels at it. The pellets struck the chimney like a sandstorm, but once again the bird wasn't hit. It raised its large, deformed wings, made some choppy movements in the air and then floated away like a black, whooshing shadow into the trees.

So I'd missed it a second time – and this time from only six or seven yards away. I don't understand what's wrong with me. Can my hands really have gotten so unsteady?

Aug. 9. I was woken up several times last night by Bella's restlessness. Apparently she couldn't sleep. She moved around constantly; a couple of times I heard the sound of her paws on the floor. At three o'clock my sleep was interrupted by loud, persistent growling. I sat up in bed and lit a match. She was standing by the door in a tense, watchful attitude, *growling at something that was right outside the house at that very moment*. I got up. I wasn't fully awake; my eyes were bleary and almost blind with sleepiness, but I managed to light the lamp and grabbed the first weapon I could find, a stick. Then I pushed the door open and went out. There was no one outside, everything was quiet. A calm night wind whispered through the treetops, slight like the sound of the ocean in a seashell. I called out once and heard the sound of my own voice rolling through the woods. But no one answered.

The hell with that dog! I'm really starting to get annoyed with Bella now. She's making me anxious. If this keeps up, I may have to shoot her.

In the morning I got another glimpse of the crow, but this time it flew away before I had the chance to take a shot at it. It knows me now and isn't taking any more chances. Incidentally, I made a curious discovery: *the bird only has one leg*, the right one is missing. Maybe my first shot got it after all? I don't know, but I've suddenly been struck by a strange thought. I've just remembered what the sheriff told me about Tore Gruvik: that he was missing his right foot. That doesn't mean anything in and of itself, it's just a silly and meaningless association of thoughts. Only I don't understand why it bothers me so much – I've been thinking about it all day . . .

Aug. 10. Had a strange dream last night. I'm standing on the shore of Blue Lake. It's a moonlit night, and I'm watching a lily floating on the surface. It's bright and pure, with the cool, perfect whiteness of the moon; it's wonderfully beautiful. While I'm looking at it, captivated by the sight, it slowly glides under a tall spruce tree that's growing on the shore, leaning over the lake at an angle so that it casts a black reflection in the water. Just when the lily comes into the tree's shadow, it starts to wilt; the lovely white crown-shaped petals slowly curl up, wither, turn a filthy gray color. While this is happening, I feel a wild and irresistible urge to jump from the shore, to grab the flower and sink to the bottom with it. Finally I throw myself in – an exquisite, frenzied leap – grab the lily, feel the water closing over my head, feel myself sinking, sliding down into a blurry, bluish darkness . . .

In the morning I walk to the lake and sit there for almost two hours, looking down into the water. I don't know why I do it; it's a mood, a whim, an irresistible urge. As I sit there, I fall into a sleeplike state, a sort of narcosis. The contours of the world around me disappear; I see nothing but my own reflection flickering deep down in the blue-green water. Is it dangerous to stare into such a lake? Isn't there an old adage that says you shouldn't stop in the woods to look? If you stay a moment too long, you'll see Pan, and those who see Pan go insane.

I have to break away from the spell by force. I feel strange and lifeless in my own body. I walk back to the cabin at a brisk march and make myself a cup of strong coffee. Tomorrow I'll stay inside and read all day; there's no reason I have to go outside. After all, I had planned to spend my time reading these first few weeks before the hunting season starts . . .

Aug. 11. I had an odd dream again last night. I'm on the steps of a train, looking out on a long, narrow country road that leads to the station. Suddenly I see a woman running along this road. She's being followed. Her face shows every sign of terror – her pursuer is gaining on her. I don't know who she is, but by a sudden inspiration I call her name: 'Beatrice!' She sees me and comes running towards me; I channel all my willpower into her reaching the train before she's overtaken. And she makes it just in time. I reach out for her and pull her into the train. She collapses exhausted at my feet, and just then the train begins to move . . .

. . . An incomprehensible urge has sprung up in me, a monstrous desire, an impulse the likes of which I've never known. *It takes a violent effort to pull myself together and not go to the lake.* I lock the cabin door, put the key in my pocket, and force myself to lie quietly in bed with a book. Bella paces restlessly back and forth across the floor; she must feel that something is wrong with her master. What is it pulling me out there? My head hurts, my body burns as if from a secret fever. I feel an overwhelming desire just to walk to the door, unlock it, and go out for a while. But thank goodness I have strength of character.

I won't go out there. I won't!

Aug. 12. Did I say strength of character? Today I did go out. I couldn't control myself any longer; it was impossible, I *had* to go. I sit for hours again today staring down into the water. I get a deep and painful sense of well-being from it; it's like giving in to a disgusting vice and at the same time conducting a fantastic experiment. Yes, it's like I'm experimenting with secret, unknown forces, forces beyond life and death. It's like I'm touching a great curtain, the veil concealing the ultimate mystery. Maya's veil!*

As I sit there, I hear the heavy beating of wings from a large bird coming closer. I hear it in the air above me, I glimpse its shadow gliding over the water. It lands in one of the trees on the other side of the lake. I don't look up, but I know it's the crow. It's sitting there staring at me, looking at me with its evil, human eyes. I know it, I know it . . . Then the dreadful thing happens.

My reflection in the water starts to change shape. The body transforms, becomes broader, more robust; the arms are longer, apelike. The facial features are erased and slowly take on new contours: high cheekbones, a low, brutish forehead falling back at an angle from the eyebrows, a mouth with narrow, cruel lips. A red beard covers the lower half of the face, shooting out like flames from the chin and cheeks. And the foot! One foot is missing, the right. The leg ends a little below the knee; instead of a foot there's a short stick, a wooden leg –

The reflection I am staring at is no longer my own!

A scream escapes from my chest; it comes like an explosion from my throat. I get up and run, run back to the house, desperate with terror. I stumble over my own feet, I fall and get up again, keep running, my heart beating like an ax against my ribs.

Behind me I hear the crow calling after me, mocking me.

Aug. 13. I've just read what I've written in my diary the past few days. I must have been mad; I don't understand myself anymore. But today my mind is clear, and today I've made my decision: I'm going back to Oslo tomorrow. I can't stay here any longer. I have to get away from here, out of these woods. I'll pack my backpack tonight.

Sitting here looking out the window, I feel like I'm in

a fortress. Somewhere out in the woods is the enemy, the invisible foe. He's lying still, waiting, watching me; I'm under siege. But I'll play a trick on him, I'll cheat him of his prey. I'll make a lightning-fast retreat. Tomorrow I'll leave; yes, tomorrow I'll leave.

Aug. 14. No, I can't leave. He's seen through me, he's figured out my plan. *He won't let me escape.* The moment I stepped out the cabin door this morning, I heard a bird's hoarse shriek coming from the edge of the woods. It was the crow, sounding the alarm. Look, he's trying to escape! it shrieked. Stop him! And it felt as though something were blocking the road in front of me. I couldn't take a step in the right direction, the road to the village; there was only one direction I could move: *towards the lake!*

Bella whined and tugged at me to get me to move. I stumbled, my vision went dark, my blood pounded through my veins. If I had remained outside a few seconds longer I don't know what would have happened. I summoned my last reserves of strength, rushed into the house again, pulling Bella along with me, and locked the door.

No, I can't leave. All day long I've paced restlessly back and forth, like a prisoner in his cell. I see the woods surrounding me like a shackle. The branches weave together, forming bars, a ring that gets tighter and tighter. I'm sealed in, there's no hope of escape –

Aug. 15. Yes! I know it: he's here in the room, here now, at this moment. I don't see him, but I sense his presence. I feel his frozen breath, hear the beating of his dead heart. The water streams from his face, falling in thick, green drops onto his clothes. His eyes are like open, running sores under his low forehead. They stare at me, they're the color of the lake – yes, they're the lake's eyes! He whispers to me through his white lips. I killed myself, he whispers. I killed myself the night of August 22 . . .

I keep him at bay by talking to myself aloud continuously. I carry on a conversation with myself about some ridiculous subject, the latest news in the publishing industry, the prospects of good weather, the price of potatoes, God knows what. I *must* talk to someone, I can't stand being alone in this place any longer. I have to see a living person, a person of flesh and blood. This terrible solitude is driving me insane, yes, insane!

Aug. 16. 3:00 p.m.

Today I caught him off guard, I escaped! Early this morning I got up, and without packing my backpack, without eating breakfast, barely dressed, I went out and started to run down the road. I was blind, deaf, I didn't feel anything, I just ran – several miles without stopping. And I made it! The force possessing me must have loosened its grip, and I broke free. After an hour and a half alternately running and briskly walking I was down in the village. I went straight to Sheriff Bråten's house. He's the only person I know here; besides, he has strong nerves, a calming presence. I wanted to see *him*.

He wasn't home. As I stood outside waiting, I was struck by the ridiculousness of the situation. What had I done? Hadn't I fled like a frightened rabbit, run away from my luggage, my dog, my gun, and everything else? What sort of man was I, anyway? Bråten would laugh in my face.

And then I thought of something else: *I had betrayed my great experiment!* Wasn't I standing before an unfathomable secret? Hadn't I touched the veil the other day, seen into the hidden world? Hadn't I been an outpost at the border of that unknown land? Why should I pull back now? Was I a coward?

I left a card in the mailbox, using some excuse or other

to ask him to come and see me tomorrow; maybe I'll need him then. Was that a sign of weakness? Yes, it was. But in any case I went back. Yes, I went back to the cabin!

I'm not scared anymore. I have the courage of a sleep-walker; I feel prepared for anything, whatever may come. Shouldn't I fight back? Against whatever's out there?

No, I'm no coward.

11:00 p.m.

I shouldn't have come back. My God, I should have stayed down there! Now I'm in his power! Now he'll never let me go. He's sharpened his lookout; the crow is sitting on the chimney directly above my head. Through the fire-place I can hear the clawing sound of its one foot scraping against the stones. Haha, now he's got me!

He's standing at the door; I feel him standing at the door, looking at me, cold and merciless. Oh, that look! He stands motionless in the shadows, his arm raised. He points into the woods, towards the lake. The water runs off him, vis-cous, slimy, like from secret, loathsome glands –

I can't resist any longer – my blood is turning black in my veins – shadows are falling over my eyes – no, I can't – can't –

Why?

Why should I resist?

I have to know what happens – down there in the dark-ness – when it closes over me – I must go out there – to the lake – take the plunge – the plunge – yes!

My great experiment?

I'm coming.

CHAPTER SIX

In which Sonja goes for a swim

WERNER'S DIARY MADE THE ROUNDS; we took turns reading it, and there's no denying it made a rather strong impression on us. As might be expected, Liljan in particular was greatly affected. I noticed she gradually grew paler as she read; when she finally put the book down, her face was almost ashen. Her glance fluttered helplessly around the room. Her lips were bloodless and quivering; she looked as though she were freezing. I felt truly sorry for her. It had been a terrible blow, this business with her brother, and now she was getting this grotesque description of the tragedy into the bargain.

Sonja, who is as kind and compassionate a person as I am, put a reassuring arm around Liljan's shoulder and led her outside into the sunshine. You could tell she needed a little fresh air. The rest of us remained seated for a while, looking at each other.

'Well?' Bugge said finally. 'What do you think about all of this?'

'To be honest, I think it all seems pretty creepy,' I said. 'It's not exactly uplifting reading. It reminds me of a horror story by Poe or Hanns Heinz Ewers. I didn't think that sort of thing happened to people in real life – '

'I find the text extremely interesting,' Mørk declared. 'I'd like to get permission to print it in its entirety in the next issue of *The Scourge*, which will deal with the relationship between the self and evil spirits. It's been a long time since I've read anything as wonderful as this. There's something

Russian about the whole description, you can't help but think of Andreyev. If you recall what I wrote in my article "Russian Death Poetry of the Nineteenth Century" – '

'That doesn't have a damn thing to do with it,' Bugge interrupted sharply. 'You haven't come up here to write your dissertation on "Literary Influences of Suicide Victims". All I want to know is whether any of you found anything in this diary, anything striking, which might bring us closer to an explanation.'

I thought about it.

'Yes,' I said. 'There was something that struck me. These dreams Werner refers to are remarkably similar to your anonymous patient's. Maybe that's because Bjørn Werner was your patient? Is that why you're so interested in – ?'

I stopped short when I noticed Bugge's facial expression. He was giving me a look that told me loud and clear to shut up. I realized it was a mistake to mention it in the presence of the others; Bugge takes his patients' confidentiality very seriously and now here I was, making him look like just another blabbermouth. There was an awkward silence for a few seconds, during which I wished the floor would open up and swallow me. Then Gran got up from his seat, holding the diary open in front of him.

'If I may, I'd like to offer a little hypothesis,' he said. 'It's possible it'll sound a bit strange.'

'Well?' Bugge looked up at him with curiosity.

'I'm of the opinion that it *wasn't* our late friend who wrote the last part of this diary.'

'Who else could it have been?'

'The man or woman who murdered Bjørn Werner.'

Gran's voice was steady. And he had the same gleam in his eyes that Archimedes must have had when he leapt out of the bathtub.

'These pages were written to make Werner's suicide seem more plausible and to make everything fit with the old legend. Any of us who knew Werner knows that he *couldn't* have been responsible for such melodramatic nonsense.'

Bugge gave his friend an approving look.

'So you're sticking to your murder theory. You really have my respect, Gran. I think you have the makings of a great scientist; you have the genius's predilection for finding absolutely the most improbable solution to every problem. What do you base your theory on?'

'It's very simple.' Gran laid the diary on the table in front of Bugge. 'First of all, notice that where the month of August begins, there are a number of pages torn out. On August 1, Werner went up to the cabin; rather striking that pages should be torn out right there, isn't it? Next, look at the handwriting. *It's not the same in July and August.* The T's and D's are different after August 1, likewise the F's and R's. You see the discrepancy especially well if you compare the writing on the final pages with the writing in the first part of the book. The imitation of Werner's handwriting is good, but not good *enough*. A trained eye can see through the forgery. What Werner himself wrote in August has been torn out and replaced with what you've just read.'

Bugge leafed back and forth in the book and examined the characters through a magnifying glass Gran lent him. A couple of times he shook his head and frowned. Finally he looked up.

'You're completely certain?'

'Absolutely.' Gran gave a becomingly modest smile. 'Graphology is my specialty as a criminal investigator.'

'Let's try and summarize your theory. So you think a murderer travels up here in the dead of night, kills Werner and his dog, learns someone else's handwriting on short notice and writes a short story *à la* Poe on the fly, goes down to the village and delivers a cryptic note, puts on Werner's shoes and carries his corpse to the lake, where he throws him in – only to leap up in the air and disappear thereafter; after all, the footsteps do end, if I remember correctly, at the edge of the lake. That's your explanation, right?'

'Something along those lines,' Gran replied drily. 'Something along those lines, my dear friend.'

'Nick Carter,' exclaimed Mørk, turning an imploring look towards the heavens. 'Good God, Nick Carter must be rolling over in his grave.'

Just then Sonja stuck her head through the window. The one facing the veranda was open.

'Why don't we go and check out the lake?' she said. 'I'm so anxious to see it.'

We went out into the sunshine and sauntered along the road at a leisurely pace, all six of us. The woods around us seemed dark and dense by day too; the light coming through the tall trunks was fairly scant. Somebody once told me that you could fit the world's entire population on the island of Bornholm, but if so, they'd presumably have to be standing as close together as the trees in those woods.

Meanwhile the shimmering August sky hung high above our heads. The air still had the soft aroma of summer and was filled with the chirping of birds and the gentle humming of insects. Even reading Werner's macabre descriptions hadn't shaken my opinion that it was a lovely day.

'I don't understand how Werner could write that there were no birds here,' I said. 'It's teeming with songbirds now, anyway. On the other hand, I haven't seen any sign of the crow – that ghost bird which, according to his account, should be the only one in the woods.'

'That proves what I was just saying – the diary is a fake,' declared Gran. 'Those descriptions are just for effect, intended to frighten the reader. Of course Werner found songbirds here. And of course he never saw any such ghost crow.'

'Be careful about drawing hasty conclusions,' Bugge

objected. 'I'm not at all certain the diary was forged –
despite your expert opinion. There's a strange inner logic
in the description of how he's slowly sucked in by the lake,
by madness – a logic that makes me think we're dealing
with a completely genuine account. And that view is confirmed by just those sorts of details, such as his neither
hearing nor seeing any living birds here, only a ghost bird,
an invulnerable and immortal crow with one leg, Tore
Gruvik in animal form.'

'Now I think you're starting to go occult on us. Or
maybe you'd care to explain yourself a little better?'

'With pleasure. Werner's depiction proves that his sensory impressions were different from ours; he heard and
saw something different from us. Everything points to the
fact that he went mad in the course of those two weeks.
And can we expect a mentally ill person to have the same
sensory impressions, the same image of reality, as we
normal people? Of course not. A psychopath will always
have a totally different image; *fantasy* will be his reality,
the exterior world only scenery, a background. Of course
things didn't objectively happen in the way described in the
diary. But they did happen that way subjectively, in his own
brain, in his fantasy. Think about how we experience the
world during a fever. What is hallucination and what is a
real sensory impression? In the end, the mind is our only
reality.'

'It's blasphemy when a materialist dares to use that sort
of expression,' Mørk contended. 'It's like hearing a waiter
give his thoughts on Michelangelo.'

Mørk had already shown signs several times of wanting
to jump into the discussion, but he couldn't get a word in
edgewise with Bugge and Gran. Now his face was flushed
from his pent-up arguments, now he *had* to speak.

'Your entire analysis shows that you don't understand
a thing about the life of the mind, the life of the soul,'

he continued. 'You have as much right to call yourself a depth psychologist as a tourist to the Danish seaside has to call himself an oceanographer. You go on and on about psychopathy and sensory impressions and hallucinations; it sounds like a high school science lecture, nothing but disconnected abstractions, empty scientific formulas that don't mean anything. Why not call things by their right names? Why not accept Werner's own explanation: that he was possessed by an evil spirit?'

'Sorry,' said Bugge. 'But for the time being, science must reject the existence of evil spirits. Unfortunately we must also refrain from believing in Santa Claus.'

'There you have it!' Mørk shouted triumphantly. 'You don't even believe in Santa Claus! That's how far science has come in sterilizing our ideas, that's how poor it's made us. Getting rid of God and Satan wasn't enough, it wasn't enough to deprive the universe of its soul; you'd also wipe out what little remains of our humanity – you'd do away with Santa Claus! And science demands that we believe in its own completely unimaginative constructs, its childish fable of the world as a modern mechanical toy with clockwork and gears delivered straight from Meccano. No, you can keep your science for yourselves, gentlemen. I subscribe to Nils Kjær's excellent definition of science: "Some old local doctors sitting around discussing materialism".'

'In other words, you believe Werner was really possessed by Tore Gruvik's spirit?' I said – and tried to say it slightly ironically, so it wouldn't sound too naive.

'Of course. Is it really possible for a thinking person – I say a *thinking* person – not to believe in spirits? Open any modern novel, delve down into the puddle of urges, of sordid instincts, of black magic, witches' sabbaths and Walpurgis nights – you'll find possessed people everywhere. They're possessed by evil spirits, by demons – proper demons like you see depicted in medieval paintings;

back then people were more realistic in their conception of reality – they're possessed, I say, because they have no sense of self, no power within them that can withstand the evil. The world opens up beneath them, and they plunge into the abyss like Korah and his followers in the Book of Numbers. That's the way our friend Bjørn Werner went. He was a child of our cultural dark age . . .'

We had arrived at the lake. It lay like an oval, blue-green mirror framed between the trees; the surface was totally still and gave the impression of something completely lifeless. Here and there a few water lilies floated with a strangely frozen, fossilized appearance; they looked like ice flowers on a windowpane. Along the shore some brown, rotten tree stumps protruded, their muddy branches splaying through the pale green reeds like the fingers of a drowned troll. A cool breeze was coming off the water's shining surface, a column of cold that rose straight up through the warm autumn air. It was like suddenly being in a different season.

We stood on a small plateau about a yard above the surface, a little ledge with the deep water right in front of it, presumably the spot where the sheriff had found Werner's footprints. At other parts of the shore it was evidently shallow for several yards out; reeds were growing there tight and lush like an Amazon forest. As I stood looking down at the water, I felt a hint of what Werner had described: the pull, the invisible maelstrom somewhere down below. I shivered despite myself, a little chill went through me. *He* was down there in the depths, our friend. Here was where he had thrown himself in; here a wild and unfathomable impulse had dragged him down into the darkness.

I looked up and happened to see Liljan, who was standing beside me. I was shocked. She looked like a medium in a trance, a hypnotized person. She was staring straight ahead of her with a fixed look; her mouth was half-open and had an apathetic expression. I grabbed her arm. It was stiff, the muscles tense and quivering as though in a spasm.

'Liljan!' I said. 'Are you ill? Is something the matter?'

It was like she'd been woken up with a slap. In the course of a second she lost that strange, sleepwalker-like attitude. She looked down, ashamed, as though she had been caught in the act doing something illegal. I had the feeling I was the only one who had seen her in that condition. She had been away for a moment and had come back to reality. Where had she been? An unpleasant thought struck me. Maybe Werner had been in the same state? Maybe that's how he had looked when he . . .

Liljan laughed – a little forced, I thought.

'No,' she said. 'There's nothing the matter with me. It's just that – there's something that – yes, there's something so odd – '

'What kind of nonsense is this, Liljan? You're extremely pale.' Gran put his arm around her. 'What is it that's so odd?'

'You'll only think it's ridiculous – '

'Not at all. Out with it.'

'It's just a feeling I have. I have a feeling that – '

'That what?'

'That I've been here before.'

These words came simply and softly, but they had a remarkably strange sound, a sound of something unreal, something unknown. It sounded like she was amazed to hear herself saying that sort of thing.

'But *have* you been here before, then? With your brother, for example?'

'No, I've never been here. And yet I *have*, that's what's so odd. I recognize it – the trees over there – the rotten trunks sticking up at an angle from the water – the five lilies form-ing a half circle – yes, I recognize it. I don't understand – '

'It's just a touch of nerves,' said Gran, pressing her to

him more tightly. 'You're upset because of what happened to your brother. Besides, no doubt you have seen a lake like this before; I certainly can't tell the difference between one woodland lake and another. Isn't there something called *fausse reconnaissance* – when you imagine you've lived through something before? I think I read about it in Schjelderup's textbook back when I failed my exams.'

I noticed that Bugge was observing Liljan. He was regarding her with that squinting look of his; his face had assumed an analytical expression, as it usually does when he's looking at someone who interests him. Unfortunately, I don't have any particular knowledge of human nature myself, but I've always felt there must be something about the people Bugge is interested in. And now it suddenly struck me that there really was something odd about this girl, something mysterious; up till then I had taken her for a completely ordinary person with no serious cultural interests aside from jazz and silk stockings. She had always been overshadowed by her eccentric brother; she had been just as blessedly insignificant and refreshingly banal as any other young girl who had been born and raised in the suburbs. But now she had taken on a new dimension: she had become *interesting*. It was like she was revealing a whole new side of herself, and yet there was something she was hiding, she had a secret . . .

I looked around for Sonja and found to my surprise that she had disappeared. It turned out she had taken a little detour in the woods; thirty seconds later she stepped out daintily from between the trees – in her bathing suit. My wife's body can stand up to the most critical analysis, with or without a swimsuit, and she was an uncommonly attractive sight with her soft, slender Venus lines enclosed in the latest model Figgjo. Nevertheless I was a little startled by the sudden and unexpected sight of my wife acting like a forest nymph.

'Good lord,' I exclaimed. 'What's gotten into you? Were you thinking you'd drown yourself now and get it over with, or have you just turned into an exhibitionist?'

'I've always dreamed of bathing in an enchanted lake,' said Sonja. 'And now I want to find out how it really feels.'

She walked up to the ledge and prepared to dive in.

'You're crazy,' I said. 'Even if that ghost doesn't drag you to the bottom, you'll wind up getting a cramp; there's no way that water is over 40 degrees. Besides, we have a bathtub at home.'

Sonja didn't answer; she made a fluid movement, a graceful little leap, and vanished headfirst into the water. A wreath of green foam formed behind her. Thick, cloudy bubbles broke out over the surface; it was like pouring seltzer into a glass of absinthe. A little whirlpool, a maelstrom, formed where she had dived in, and the bubbles were mercilessly sucked down through a hole in the water. A sliver of wood also got caught in it; it tipped over the edge and was pulled down into the darkness. Kind of funny that I noticed something like that. When you're in a certain kind of mood you can often see something new and different in things, something symbolic.

My wife swims like a dolphin, and one of the things she enjoys most is swimming underwater. Now she'd been gone for a long time, almost thirty seconds, and I started to worry about her. But finally her blond head popped up thirty or forty yards from shore.

'It's wonderful!' she called, waving a wet arm.

'Enjoy yourself!' I called back.

Bugge turned towards me.

'I think you've been pretty lucky in your choice of a wife,' he said. 'She has a number of exceptional qualities you don't have. For one thing, she's *brave*.'

'Well,' I said, offended, 'if it's a question of courage, I've often taken cold showers at home myself.'

'I agree that Sonja's a brave woman,' Gran said with a smile. 'If I had tried that, I would have sunk like a stone – I can't swim.'

'You can't swim?'

'No, I'm afraid not. I must have been absent from school the day they were teaching it.'

Sonja was swimming back again, doing a front crawl. Her supple arms took long, vigorous strokes; she shot forward like a torpedo along the water's surface. But as I stood watching her, it struck me that there was something in what Bugge had said. This wasn't an ordinary bathing spot, wasn't some idyllic beach with music playing and a nice reef in the background. It wasn't normal water she was swimming in, but a strange liquid, a new and dangerous element; this was *the lake of the dead*. Sonja was brave – that was the right word.

I stood there thinking that if I could paint, this would have made a splendid picture. The contrast between life and death – a woman alone in a totally barren landscape, swimming in a lake; there's a sort of creature that surrounds her, an amorphous, jellylike creature with no shape or contours. It clings to her with its wet polyp arms, sticks to her warm white limbs, wants to catch her, immobilize her, kill her. But she overcomes her adversary, glides forward. She toys with the enemy, it's the game of life and death. Woman and death – wasn't that the theme the old painters always centered on?

Sonja had returned to the shore again. I reached out a hand and pulled her up.

'Not so bad,' she said, shaking the water off. 'But a little bit cold.'

It was obvious it had been cold. Her teeth were chattering and there was a little waft of cold air coming off her body. I started to rub some warmth into her.

'No more of these little swims from now on,' I said

sternly. 'I have no intention of being a widower until you're old and ugly.'

We walked back to the cabin again a few minutes later, talking animatedly about this and that. Mørk and Bugge were at each other's throats again, but I couldn't hear what they were saying. I didn't feel as cheerful and good-humored anymore after our visit to the lake; I had experienced something of the mood from Werner's diary. Could there really be any doubt that the diary was genuine?

I felt as if a powerful hand had suddenly grabbed my chest and shaken me out of equilibrium. It wasn't so much what I had felt at the sight of the lake as what I had read for a moment in Liljan's face. Her expression had scared me. There was something abnormal and inhuman about it, something dead and at the same time grotesquely alive; it was like a glimpse into a whole other reality. And what was it she had said? 'I have the feeling I've been here before.' It sounded so damned eerie when she said those words.

The thought of going back to Oslo occurred to me again. I had a hunch something was going to happen, something we wouldn't have any control over. Why not retreat while there was still time? Besides, was there any reason for us to stay? Wasn't this whole undertaking thoroughly point-less? But I knew such a proposal would be rejected with contempt. And at the same time I felt just the tiniest tingle of curiosity. I recognized that from Werner's book too; I remembered his words, they described my own mood. There was some unfathomable mystery before us, hidden behind a veil. Once you've touched such a veil, there's no longer any escape; you have to stay put and await your fate.

And I had already touched the veil.

CHAPTER SEVEN

In which something really starts to happen

I'VE JUST READ THROUGH what I've written up till now, and I realize I've given my readers poor value for their money. In an exciting, well-constructed crime novel, the first murder should come – if not at the bottom of page 2 – at the very least by the top of page 3, and then more murders should follow one after the other like pearls on a string. A thriller costing four kroner must under no circumstances contain fewer than four murders, which gives the reader a return of about a krone per murder on their investment. But it's not looking good for this book. We're already on page 75, and so far only a single person has met his end – and it's not even clear it was a murder. I can certainly understand how the audience must feel cheated.

I'm sorry I've chosen to present the story in this way, but it was necessary. What happened to us during those days didn't happen suddenly; it was something that developed slowly, little by little. Aside from Werner's disappearance, there were no external events in the beginning; all that occurred was an imperceptible change in our mood. In some way we became *ready* for something to happen, something inevitable. At least that's how it felt to me.

The first real event, the first fantastic incident, took place that night, the night of August 20.

Gran spent the morning conducting a systematic search of the entire cabin, while the rest of us played the role of spectators. As far as I know, he didn't find anything of interest. That afternoon he took the initiative of exploring the area, a thorough reconnaissance of the vicinity. Bugge and I went with him while Liljan and Sonja stayed behind to tend to dinner. Mørk refused to accompany us. He'd always been against playing cops and robbers, he said, and he preferred to stay put and examine the contents of the library.

We found a narrow path heading east, a thin crack through the woods that led to the little river. I hadn't been able to get used to the noise from that river. A soldier can get used to cannon fire on the front lines, but there are certain sounds a person simply can't get comfortable with. It was a sinister hissing sound, like a snake slithering through the grass. And even the running water had something unwholesome about it, something slimy; it reminded me of the lake water. It was funny how everything here seemed to be related, had a common touch of repulsiveness . . .

We continued along the shore a little way and stopped a couple of minutes later in front of a little hut, one of the small shanties Bråten had talked about. It was an ancient house, a ruin, certainly much older than our own residence, which wasn't exactly an example of modern architecture. The roof was covered with yellowed grass several inches tall, and the walls were almost black, not from paint, but from age. I tried to peer in through a sort of windowpane, but it was completely opaque, covered with geological layers of dust.

'This is quite a find,' I said. 'It deserves a place at the ethnographic museum, right next to the Viking ship.'

Gran pushed on the door. It seemed at first to be locked, but then it suddenly jerked open on creaking hinges. We looked into a cold and bare little room. Everything was in a woolen darkness, almost as if a gray curtain had been hung over the window. We stepped over the threshold and went in. I walked straight into a sticky veil of spiderwebs, one of the things I hate worst of all. I cursed aloud and wiped it off. Bugge laughed.

'Almost like breaking into an Egyptian tomb,' he said. 'Beware of Pharoah's vengeance.'

Dusk had already fallen outside and only a faint light came into the room; it was hard to see anything in there. Gran pulled out a pocket flashlight and switched it on. A powerful cone of light slid over the uneven, rotted floorboards and stopped at a pile of sticks and branches in one corner of the room. Gran walked over to it and bent down. He rummaged around a little in the heap and finally pulled out what proved to be an old handsaw, dark brown with rust. He stood examining his find in silence for almost a minute.

'Well?' Bugge said impatiently. Gran looked up.

'Someone's been here fairly recently.'

'Oh? How do you figure that?'

'This saw has fresh scratches in the rust. And this branch was recently sawed off. Look for yourself. The cut is fresh.'

Bugge took a superficial look at what Gran showed him.

'Very possible. After all, there certainly has been someone here as recently as yesterday. Our friend, the sheriff – '

' – is certainly not going around sawing off tree branches. And there haven't been any loggers around here lately either.'

'*Aha*. I understand. Then there's only one alternative left. The *murderer* was here, right? The killer sawed off this branch in order to make himself a club, a murder weapon. My compliments, Sherlock Holmes. Your powers of deduction are without equal.'

Gran ignored his friend's sarcasm.

'Indeed. It's extremely likely that a murderer was here. The only person we know for certain to be here in the woods is, in fact, a murderer. And an insane murderer at that.'

I gave an involuntary shudder when Gran mentioned

that. I had totally forgotten what Bråten had told us – that we had someone like that nearby! A homicidal maniac, a suicidal maniac – God help me, what kind of place had I wound up in . . .

An idea suddenly struck me.

'Isn't it possible that this notorious criminal has something to do with Werner's death?' I asked.

Gran was going to say something but checked himself. A branch snapped just outside the hut.

We stood quietly for several moments staring at each other. Then Bugge broke the silence.

'One of the others probably followed us,' he said.

I ran out with Gran at my heels. There was no one there. But the back wall of the hut was right up against the underbrush, and the sound had apparently come from that side.

'Hello!' I called. 'Sonja! Liljan! Mørk! Hello!'

No one answered. Not a sound could be heard except for the slight rustle of the trees and the murky, unwholesome noises coming from the river.

Gran shrugged his shoulders. 'It must have been an animal,' he muttered. 'A rabbit or something.'

But I saw from his face that he wasn't entirely sure. As for me, I was convinced of something else. The branch that had cracked was large, and something heavy had stepped on it. It hadn't been a rabbit's paw, it had been a human foot.

We visited two more shanties further on before making our way down the road again. Both looked just about like the first and seemed to be used as storage for tools, maybe also as primitive lodging for woodcutters. There was nothing to be found in them aside from some used matches, which Gran, with the air of an expert, declared had been there for several years.

On the way back Gran suggested we should also check out the caves Bråten had mentioned. He had spotted a couple of them along the riverbank. They were fairly small and partly camouflaged with grass and moss, but easily large enough for a person to crawl into. Bugge refused. He'd had enough for today, he said. True, he had been a boy scout in his day, but the caves would have to wait until another time. What's more, he'd suddenly gotten an irresistible appetite for dinner . . .

As we walked down, I tried to call Werner's features to mind. I'd never really gotten a handle on him; he'd been the introverted type, and his life had been on a totally different plane from mine. By and large he'd seemed friendly enough, I had liked him. What was that weird stuff Mørk had been going on about that morning, by the way? That Werner couldn't resist the evil powers because he had no sense of self? As a rule I don't understand a single thing Mørk says; I have to sit with a dictionary of foreign words open on my lap if I want to follow along with his monologues. There was one thing I was secretly sure of: Gran was wrong. Werner hadn't been killed – at least not by any living being.

'Have you actually found a motive for your murder theory?' I asked Gran. 'I still can't get my head around the idea of someone wanting to kill a guy like Werner.'

'I'm not so sure. The most inoffensive people are often a murderer's favorite target. Besides, Werner wasn't all that inoffensive.'

'What do you mean?'

'I mean there were things about him that were – well, that were fairly objectionable. And not just objectionable, for that matter. Some of them were downright disgusting.'

'What are you saying? What things?' I stared at him in astonishment.

'Among other things he was – well, anyway, maybe we should show a little respect. If not for the dead, then at least for the living. I am engaged to his sister after all.'

'Didn't you like him?'

'No, God knows I didn't.'

The conversation had taken a surprising turn. Gran had suddenly gotten emotional; his face had gone red and his hands were clenched into fists. I'd never seen him like this before. What was going on?

'But listen here – ' I was interested now – 'let's say Werner did have his bad side; if so, I must have overlooked it – the only people in the world I don't like are waiters and tax collectors. Even so, it's quite a leap to go from that to murdering him, isn't it? I've never killed a waiter, for example, though I'll admit I do have one man at Blom's restaurant in my sights.'

I tried to think of a hypothetical question that might get him talking. And found it.

'Is it possible, for instance, that one of us up here had a reason to kill him?'

There was a noticeable pause after I said that. Gran didn't seem to want to answer.

'Well, what do you think?'

'As I recall, Werner once spoke derisively about *The Scourge*,' Bugge interjected. 'So in a sense you might say Mørk had a motive.'

Bugge clearly liked making fun of Gran's theories. But Gran apparently took it as a serious contribution.

'Mørk?' he said. 'Funny you should mention Mørk of all people. Did either of you actually see him between the first and the sixteenth of August?'

Bugge shook his head. I thought about it.

'No,' I admitted. 'Why? You don't think – ?'

'I don't think anything. I'm just considering a number of possibilities.'

Gran still had a rather peculiar look on his face. His voice seemed a little strange too. Bugge took a cigarette from his pocket and lit it carelessly.

'If Mørk were going to resort to murder,' he said, 'I think he would prefer to do away with a modern novelist. Sigurd Hoel,* for example. Or Aksel Sandemose.* Or why not Bernhard Borge?'

We met Sonja, who came bearing two buckets; she had been down to the river to get water. I chivalrously helped her carry them, and she and I fell a little behind the others. I saw right away there was something on her mind.

'You know, Bernhard,' she said, 'I'm actually starting to get a little worried.'

'Worried? About what?'

'About Liljan. She's not herself anymore. She's terribly upset.'

'Is she? Yes, I noticed her down by the lake this afternoon. She's always been a little high-strung. And now this business of her brother's death . . .'

'But it's not just that, Bernhard. There's something else too. Something totally new. I have the feeling she's somehow *threatened* by something, the same feeling she had about Bjørn. You know, I'm really scared that something is going to happen to her.'

'Nonsense. What could happen to her? She's here with us. Surely you're not superstitious?'

'Oh, I don't know. But still, for the first time I'm a little frightened. I think something might happen to her. Maybe as soon as tonight . . .'

My wife's instinct is spot-on. Something did happen that night.

We got tired early that evening, no doubt due to the country air and one thing and another, and went to bed around eleven. But I didn't fall asleep as quickly as I had expected; I lay awake long after Sonja had dozed off. I had sneaked a drink from Gran's bottle before crawling into bed, and a pleasant feeling was streaming through my body. It would have been a pity to fall asleep and lose that little buzz. I lay there looking at the starry sky and the large moon, carefully framed in the upper left-hand pane; it rested just on top of the white-painted frame, looking like a silver plate on a stand. The night has an intoxicating atmosphere of its own, I thought, even in a place like this. I lay there reciting some lines of poetry to myself, something I had once read, a stanza I had loved:

> 'How sickly large was the moon
> and blue and springlike the night . . .'

The house was totally quiet. Only now and then there came a creaking from within the rotting walls, where the wood, as if in resignation, was yielding to the weight of age and collapsing in on itself. There was something melancholy about that sound; it was the sound of transience, the music of destruction. It harmonized well with the cool, sad scent of the autumn air. I felt almost elegiac lying there. If only I could write poetry!

Suddenly I pricked up my ears. I had heard a sound, a new sound, which stood out clearly from the normal creaking in the walls. There was something moving close by, something alive. It sounded like something moving across a floor.

Normally I wouldn't pay any attention to that sort of thing. There were six of us in the house, after all, and it was very likely that one of us might have some little errand to do in the course of the night. But I had been so strangely sensitive and alert the past twenty-four hours. My senses had grown sharper, I immediately reacted to the slightest impression. What's more, there was something special about that sound, something unusual; I can't explain what it was.

It was silent for a couple of seconds. I strained my ears for the slightest noise and my heart pounded with fast, nervous thumps in my chest. A strange and unexpected change had come over the atmosphere. A few moments earlier I had been in a poetic mood, letting myself be intoxicated by the moonlight and Gran's aquavit. Now something else had suddenly crept in, something I had been waiting for, something that had been in the air the whole time.

The sound came again. And this time I was able to localize it better: it was coming from Liljan's room, which shared a wall with ours. I heard footsteps on the floor in there: slow, mechanical steps towards the living room door, a soft noise that indicated it was someone walking barefoot. Then I heard a hand on the door handle, pressing it down cautiously. But the door didn't open.

Liljan! I immediately thought of what Sonja had said earlier that evening: 'I have the feeling there's something threatening Liljan. I'm afraid something is going to happen to her.' I instinctively sat up in bed and leaned my head close against the wall. I got really annoyed at my heart for barking like an excited watchdog. It was hard for me to hear over all the noise it was making.

It was silent again in the room next door. It was as though she hesitated for a moment – yes, because it couldn't be anyone other than *her* in there, could it? – like she was standing undecided in front of the door, waiting, unable to make up her mind. Maybe she was listening? Maybe she wanted to be sure that no one else was awake?

Finally I heard the faint squeak of the door sliding open; she was going out into the living room. A moment later I heard the front door open too. The veranda floor creaked, and the footsteps vanished into the night.

I don't know exactly how long I lay still in bed without doing anything. I felt an ardent curiosity in me, a burning urge to jump down to the floor and run to the window. But at the same time something held me back. The warmth of the bed, of course, but something else as well: the feeling

I would see something ghastly out there in the darkness, the fear of the unknown. I was frozen somehow, like we often are in dangerous situations requiring concentration and quick action. Maybe a minute went by before I overcame this inertia. Afterwards I realized how valuable those seconds were; if I had gotten out of bed only a few moments later it would have been too late to avert the tragedy. There's no denying that it still gives me chills when I think back on it.

I threw the blankets aside and slid to the floor, went to the window and stuck my head out. I didn't see anything in particular at first, only the soft, velvety autumn sky and the dark trees covered in a transparent veil of moonlight. I was just about to go back and creep under the warm covers again when I suddenly caught sight of something white moving along the road. It gave me a little shock. It was all I could do to stifle a scream, a cry of amazement and terror.

But let it be said to my credit that from that point on I acted fast. I ran back to the bedroom at top speed, threw on a dressing gown – my wife's morning robe, incidentally – opened the door, ran through the living room and out onto the veranda, stormed across the garden and on down the road.

Liljan was walking along the road a couple of hundred yards ahead of me. I say *walking* because language is so imprecise; really she was *gliding*, moving continuously but without any living rhythm in her body. Her golden hair fell over her shoulders; she was wearing only a thin silk nightgown, which took on a bluish-white glow in the moonlight and gave her the appearance of something immaterial, something ghostly. Her arms were stretched out in front of her the whole time and her head was raised; she moved as though in a trance. And – what had almost made me scream at first – *she was walking straight towards the lake.*

I'll never forget that minute. All around me lay the

forest, the enchanted forest with its blue depths of darkness and its storybook atmosphere; in front of me walked this woman, unreal like a fairy in the moonlight, and still further on was the lake, the lake of the dead. I could already hear sounds coming from it. It was the chorus of frogs that croaked all through the night. It sounded like a noise from the underworld.

I don't know what I was actually thinking while I ran. I was really filled with only one idea, a single thought racing through my head: I had to catch up to her before she reached the lake. I ran as fast as I could, gaining on her one yard at a time, but now the water wasn't very far off either – she was only about fifteen yards away, and there were still fifty yards separating the two of us. I yelled her name several times at the top of my lungs, but it was no good, she didn't hear me. Now the lake was right in front of her, she was walking straight for it. She stopped at the shore, groping at the air with her hands. Then she slowly fell forward – towards her own reflection . . .

I grabbed her just in time, snatched her literally in mid-fall. I was almost exhausted from the excitement and the physical exertion; I was panting like I had just run a marathon, but I still had the strength to pick her up and drag her back several yards. She offered no resistance; her body lay limp and motionless in my arms. Her face had a strange kind of frozen beauty. Her eyes were wide open, but there was no expression in them. They just stared blindly out into space; she was *asleep*. There was an odd contrast between that dead face and the living body I felt in my arms, the warm skin under that thin, rustling silk. She was really quite lovely in that grotesque state, and in that moment I was more enthralled than really scared. I think I probably stood there holding her a little longer than was strictly necessary.

But my head was immediately clear again. What had

happened was fantastic. Without being conscious of it, she had walked out here to throw herself in the lake. Purely by chance I had saved her at the last second, saved her from certain death! As I stood there observing her, it struck me that this was the very same somnambulistic attitude I'd seen a glimpse of that morning. *This* was what had been foreshadowed. She had become one of the possessed – the lake had gotten hold of her. Had Werner looked like a sleepwalker too? Maybe it was just like Bugge said: that Werner's diary held the key to the mystery. But what was the explanation for all of this? In Heaven's name, surely there had to be a sensible explanation?

I decided to wake her.

'Liljan,' I called, shaking her. 'You've got to wake up!'

She must have been in an unbelievably deep sleep, since she hadn't woken at once when I grabbed her. Nor did she wake up easily now; I had to shake her hard several times before she finally came to.

She gave me a look that expressed profound confusion, then stared with terrified, astonished eyes at the forest around us and at the lake.

'Where am I?' she whispered. 'Where am I? Someone was calling me. Someone was calling . . .'

And she looked at me again in a way that for a moment made me believe she had gone mad.

'You just went for a little walk in your sleep,' I said. 'There's nothing to worry about. Come on, let's get back to the house.'

I took her arm in mine, kindly but firmly, and she let herself be led willingly. Neither of us said anything more.

But behind us the frogs croaked in the lake, furiously and hatefully, like a gallery audience that has been cheated out of the highlight of the night's entertainment.

CHAPTER EIGHT

In which Bugge is cast in a strange light

THE OTHERS WERE AWAKENED by the noise when I ran out of the cabin, and they were all standing outside the house when Liljan and I returned. They had flung on garments in haste and looked, by and large, pretty disheveled and confused. But Liljan and I must have also been a fairly strange sight as we walked arm in arm along the road, she barefoot in a nightgown, I dressed in pajamas and my wife's bathrobe. The situation would have been funny if it hadn't been so macabre.

Sonja ran straight to her friend and took her in her arms.

'What happened?' she whispered. 'You're not hurt, are you?'

Liljan only shook her head. She looked straight ahead with a blank expression; she still seemed half asleep and didn't understand any of what was going on. She shivered with cold – not so much the night air as an inner chill, a fever. Gran pushed me gently aside and put his arm around her waist. Even in a situation like that one, I found his possessive attitude a little annoying.

We went in. Gran and Sonja bombarded me with questions. Only now did it really hit me; I was so shaken that I had a hard time expressing myself in complete sentences, but they managed to drag a sort of explanation out of me. I felt feverish chills too, a trembling throughout my whole body, as if my heart were pumping ice-cold water through my veins instead of blood. Bugge stared at Liljan intently with one of those squinting looks of his.

'The lake,' he muttered. 'The lake again. We're getting warm now.'

I didn't really get what he meant by that last remark, but I also didn't feel like thinking any more about it. I sank exhausted into a chair and greedily guzzled down a drink Gran poured for me. Sonja made Liljan drink a whole glass of aquavit, which helped. Her features relaxed again, and the life came back into her eyes. With motherly authority, Sonja made sure she went straight to bed and insisted on sleeping in the same room with her; Liljan wasn't to be left alone. It's as if my wife were born to protect and care for other people. Without comparing them in other ways, her temperament is like that of a St Bernard dog.

The other four of us sat down by the fire. Gran fetched some logs, at the same time setting a new bottle of spirits on the table – a surprise he had stashed at the bottom of his rucksack.

'I think we could all use a little pick-me-up after that,' he said as he poured the drinks. I was inclined to agree with him.

We sat for a while in silence and let the liquor take effect. A thin wisp of smoke from four cigarettes spread through the room while a lively fire crackled on the hearth in front of us. I felt that this was a sort of defensive measure; we were entrenching ourselves against whatever was out there behind a wall of *comfort*. And it worked. After the second drink, the rest of my anxiety had been washed away, leaving only a strong feeling of amazement and curiosity behind.

'What happened tonight totally defies explanation,' I began. 'I've assumed this whole time that all that stuff about Tore Gruvik and the pull of the Blue Lake was just rubbish. But now I think I'm almost starting to lean towards a belief in spiritualism.'

'I think you can safely wait a bit yet,' said Gran, as he

knocked the ash from his cigarette. 'What happened to Liljan may not be so inexplicable after all. I've known her for several years – fairly intimately, I think I might say – and I can assure you there's nothing new or surprising about her walking in her sleep. She's been a sleepwalker for as long as I've known her.'

'In other words, it's – '

' – a kind of nocturnal bad habit of hers. A fairly common habit, by the way. Some people snore, others walk in their sleep.'

'But why was she heading for the lake, of all places?'

'A coincidence. It's well known that sleepwalkers play with death; they love to balance on rooftops and enjoy doing gymnastics on balcony railings sixty feet above the pavement. I've had to intervene several times when Liljan wanted to go for a stroll on the balcony in the early morning hours. There's no question sleepwalking is a dangerous habit, considerably more dangerous than snoring.'

'But I've never heard of sleepwalkers killing themselves,' I objected. 'They're fabulous tightrope artists and never fall unless someone wakes them up. In this case Liljan tried to jump into the water *before* I woke her.'

'That's not so strange either; she's done something similar before. Recently she walked in her sleep at home in Oslo. She headed straight into the bathroom and lay down in a tub full of water – at which point she immediately woke up. It's pretty hard to sleep with water in your nose, after all. As a matter of fact, that happened the day before we came up here.'

Gran bent over and put a log on the fire.

'It's extremely unlikely that she would have drowned out there. She would have awakened as soon as the water hit her face, and as I said, she's used to being woken up like that. Besides, she swims like a fish.'

I felt reassured listening to Gran. He always keeps his

cool, and here he had immediately found a nice, simple thread in the middle of the tangle. What he said seemed quite plausible. Although maybe deep down I wasn't entirely convinced; somewhere there was something that didn't add up.

'There's no need whatsoever to get worked up and see sinister mysteries where there aren't any. In my opinion, Liljan's sleepwalking doesn't mean anything. This episode is a coincidence, plain and simple, and only seems a little eerie because we have that legend about the lake in the back of our minds. But I think we can all agree we don't believe in that old tale. Ultimately there's a natural explanation for everything.'

'Ah,' said Mørk, looking at Gran with an interested expression. 'There's a natural explanation for everything? A very original remark.'

Mørk's lips twisted into a smile that made him look like an unusually malicious caricature by Daumier.

'It's rather amusing, sitting here listening to you explain it all so sensibly,' he said. 'There's a natural explanation for everything, right. That's the formula modern man uses to solve every problem: you go about the universe with your little multiplication table, and the result is always two times two makes four. Very reasonable, but unfortunately I don't believe in so-called reason. I think that reason is the highest form of stupidity. I'm sorry, Gran, but you don't understand what's going on here any more than some Nobel Prize winner in astrophysics understands the starry sky.'

'Will you ever stop with these deranged lectures of yours?' Gran sneered angrily. Mørk ignored him.

'I'm starting to get tired of the little multiplication table. But you can't see past it. You don't have the slightest clue about the *real* laws of the universe. You're totally ignorant of the occult powers that affect mankind – the cosmic powers, the etheric forces, demons and spirits. Liljan goes out to jump in the lake. Sleepwalking, you say, a habit, a coincidence, there's a natural explanation for everything. You don't understand the most elementary phenomenon of the occult; you don't see that she's a *medium*. You keep on insisting that two and two are four. But I say two and two *aren't* four. Two and two can be any number at all, but not four!'

Bugge laughed.

'For a modern Don Quixote, you're not so mad,' he said. 'You have a fine and heroic way of tilting at windmills that really commands respect. And for once I almost agree with what you said.'

'You agree?' said Mørk, surprised. 'Then I must have expressed myself badly.'

'I agree that what happened tonight doesn't have a "natural" explanation in the conventional sense of the word. The explanation is one which we might well call occult, for that matter. I even think you're right when you say that Liljan was a medium.'

'What sort of nonsense is that?' Gran exclaimed. 'Have you gone over to the enemy? Have *you* started believing in Santa Claus too?'

'Not yet. I just think it's a little too easy to believe that things happen by coincidence. It's no coincidence that Liljan walks to the lake in her sleep; saying that she *is* a sleepwalker is no explanation at all – on the contrary, that's a problem in itself. There's undoubtedly a hidden psychological link between everything connected with this place: the Gruvik legend, Werner's disappearance, Liljan's sleepwalking – and I believe the explanation is of a very different sort from what you'd find in a mystery novel, for example. Let's not be banal, Gran. Let's at least agree to use the *big* multiplication table.'

'I don't understand where you're going with this,' Gran declared sleepily. 'It seems to me the two of you are off

in some other galaxy. But now I'm starting to get damned
tired. Nighty-night.'

We drained our glasses and went to bed.

I slept fitfully that night. I had a nightmare: a vision of
Liljan on her way to the lake. I ran after her but couldn't
reach her; I couldn't move from the spot, like I was trying to
go the wrong way on an escalator. I saw her getting closer
to the shore, slowly but surely, her arms outstretched as
though searching for something, groping for something
I couldn't see. She was no longer alone; someone else
was walking beside her, a man. He was unusually tall
and well-built, a giant, dressed in curiously old-fashioned
clothes. He hobbled as he walked; one of his legs ended in
a wooden foot. His hand had a tight grip on her shoulder;
he was leading her, pushing her straight ahead towards the
little ledge. He turned and looked at me for a moment, his
eyes black and unmoving like a frog's and protruding like
black bubbles from his white face. His hair and beard had a
greenish hue, it looked like seaweed. I heard him laughing,
but it wasn't human laughter. I recognized the sound: it
was the croaking of the frogs in the lake . . . When I awoke I
realized what I'd heard was a frog just outside my window.

I had a headache and felt rather indisposed most of the
morning. I noticed that several of the others were in the
same condition. Gran was silent and sullen and chain-
smoked like a poker player. Mørk paced around with an
utterly apocalyptic look on his face, and even Sonja, who
is usually a ray of sunshine, seemed totally out of sorts.
The conversations I tried to start every so often had something forced about them; they died away of their own
accord after a few minutes. It was almost as though we
didn't know each other already and were meeting for the
first time at a particularly awkward luncheon. The atmosphere became oppressive, and in more ways than one. The

sun blazed like it was mid-summer; the air was thick and tropical like in a greenhouse, and the old barometer on the living room wall had changed several lines over the past twenty-four hours.

Bugge was the only one who seemed totally unaffected. He sauntered around with a completely impassive expression, glancing at a book now and then, then sat down in the best chair with a look of deep contentment. Anyone who didn't know him would have taken him for a fairly ordinary guy, a lazy and snobbish good-for-nothing on a weekend trip. But I had been Bugge's friend for years and knew it meant something else: he was playing a part, his indolence was just a mask. Bugge is never more focused on a problem, never operating more intensely, than when he's lazing about in a chair and looking completely languid. And I caught a little gleam in his indolent, almost slumbering eyes: he was on watch, he was observing the others.

He didn't remain in that passive role all morning, however. Later he became active, and in a rather peculiar way: he began hitting on Liljan.

At first it looked like he just wanted to have a friendly chat, but soon I realized that he had really started flirting with her; his attitude and facial expression left no room for doubt. He leaned towards her, put his hand on her arm, talked to her in a low, intimate voice and generally behaved as though they were in the later stages of a really cozy afterparty. They sat in a corner of the living room, and I couldn't hear what they were talking about – I'm discreet by nature and had tactfully placed myself behind a book at the other end of the room. But, in any case, it seemed to me that contact had already been established between them. The flirtation was mutual; Liljan underwent a change in the span of a few minutes. Her nervous, absent-minded attitude was gone, she had relaxed, and her movements had become more graceful and vivacious. Bugge does have a reputation as a charming man; they say he has a certain grasp of the weaker sex, and now he was suddenly starting to deploy his whole technique. Subtly, of course – he's not a Latin lover from some operetta – but there was no doubt he was aiming for a conquest. Frankly I was pretty surprised. He had chosen a rather odd moment, after all.

Actually I had noticed it the day before. Liljan and Bugge had been together constantly, taking little detours several times so they could talk in private. And it had been pretty obvious that Liljan was *different* with Bugge: calmer, gentler, more feminine. But I hadn't paid much attention to it. I had chalked it up to Bugge's usual weakness for being friendly and intimate with the opposite sex; it probably didn't have any special significance. Now, though, there could be no doubt: something new was developing. And at the same time it explained why Gran had been so irritable the past twenty-four hours and so testy towards Bugge in particular. He was just plain jealous.

The more I thought about it, the clearer it became to me that a triangle had quietly formed here at the cabin. And I had the feeling Gran would get the short end of it. Usually so jovial and easygoing, he had suddenly grown grouchy and reserved. It seemed to me that a sort of scowl had come into his expression – maybe deep down he was a bit of an Othello? At any rate, he withdrew more and more from the rest of us, constantly taking solitary rambles around the area, apparently interested in nothing except his fixation: 'The Werner Murder Case'.

I felt so caught up in this new development that I completely forgot everything else that had happened the past couple of days, the atmosphere of the place, the mood from last night. But the other two didn't seem particularly interested. Sonja, who normally picks up on that sort of thing and likes to keep tabs on what her fellow women are up to, withdrew to the kitchen. And Mørk, who keeps his distance from the world's sensuality and insists that such things shouldn't exist outside Hagenbeck's zoo, had settled down on the veranda with a fountain pen and some sheets of paper. When I walked past him a few minutes later, I saw he had started a new article entitled, 'How Long Will We Still Belong to the Animal Kingdom?'

It wasn't really my intention to spy. True, I'm a curious person, but on the other hand, as I said, I'm extremely tactful and know how to mind my own business. It was almost by chance that I didn't accompany Mørk and my wife when they went for a walk along the road together half an hour later; I felt a little unwell and preferred to stay behind. I sat reading my book for a while without taking in very much of what I read; half my attention was devoted to the couple still carrying on at the other end of the room. Gran had gone out too, so it was just the three of us in the house. Suddenly I noticed Bugge giving me a sign, a little gesture indicating he wanted to be alone with Liljan. I got up, put the book under my arm, and resigned myself to leaving the room. I've always had a gentleman's sense of when my presence isn't wanted, and I've never much cared for playing the role of chaperone to my friends.

I found a nice place to lie down in front of the house and made myself comfortable, resting my head on the book. Even if nothing else came of this pointless trip, I could still treat the whole thing as a vacation and try to get a bit of a tan.

I had probably been lying there around fifteen minutes and had gotten a little drowsy from the hot sun and thick air, when I realized that something was going on inside the house. Bugge and Liljan's voices had gradually grown louder and louder. And it struck me that the voices weren't still coming from the living room, but from Liljan's bedroom. That wasn't so strange in and of itself; it was possible Bugge had made a blitz attack and was now trying to penetrate the last line of defense. But there was something about the sound of Liljan's voice that caught my attention. In the living room it had been an amorous whisper, but now it had taken on a hysterical tone. Instinctively I put my hand to my ear. It sounded as though they were having a scene.

Up to that point all I had heard of the conversation was a low murmur from inside. Now the voices had gotten sharper, clearer; I caught a word here and there. And suddenly I heard Liljan cry out, in a clear and piercing voice, 'No, no, no! I can't stand it. I don't want to do this anymore! I don't want . . .'

I stood up.

Good heavens, I said to myself. What's going on? What on earth has gotten into Bugge? It's not like him to behave like a common rapist.

Until then I had restrained myself. But now investigating further wasn't a question of simple curiosity. Now it was my *duty* to find out once and for all what was going on between those two.

I crept over to Liljan's window and cautiously peeked in through the lowest pane. Bugge had his back to me, standing totally still with his hands in his jacket pockets. Liljan was lying on the bed in front of him, her legs drawn up under her. Her voice hadn't lied; her face had a hysterical expression, her eyes wide open and almost frantic. She was staring intently at Bugge; she was in a violent emotional state, her body shaking as if from an attack of malaria.

I had been prepared for a number of possibilities, but not this one. And yet my astonishment was nothing compared to the shock I got a couple of seconds later.

Liljan suddenly leapt up from the bed, flung herself at Bugge, pressed her body desperately up against his, grabbed his jacket, and screamed:

'You . . . you . . . you want to drown me! You want to

drown me!' Then she broke into convulsive sobbing and hid her face against his chest in despair.

If the house had sunken into the earth at that very moment, I couldn't have been more astonished. My ears were buzzing, I was seeing shadows. This couldn't be real. But it *was* real. Then she raised her head again and looked at him with an expression that was furious and imploring at the same time. Bugge stood like a statue the whole time as he spoke to her in a soft and friendly tone, but I couldn't hear what he said. He was clearly trying to catch her glance, and he succeeded. She stared fixedly into his eyes, her face and body slowly untensed, and shortly afterwards she released her grip on his jacket. He laid his hand on her arm and led her gently back to the bed; she obeyed with an almost mechanical compliance.

She lay on her back in a totally relaxed position as Bugge stood leaning over her. He said something to her in a low and earnest voice, while keeping his eyes fixed the whole time on hers. It was like a veil fell gradually over her eyes. They got smaller and smaller; finally she closed them, and I immediately drew back from the window. I had seen enough and headed towards the road.

There was no question that something strange was happening to Liljan. First that little episode at the lake yesterday morning, then the sleepwalking scene last night – and finally this. I walked for a while, trying to concentrate, attempting to find an explanation, brooding over it all until my head hurt. But soon I had to give up; I couldn't find any rational connection, any tenable hypothesis.

The strangest, most uncanny thing about this latest incident was Liljan's behavior. I had always known she was high-strung and a little prone to be hysterical. Among other things, I'd been a witness to a number of milder attacks in the past. And viewed against the backdrop of what had happened last night, it wasn't all that strange that she was still pretty shaken up. What astonished and frightened me was Bugge's role in it. I had never seen him in a situation like that one before. It was an incredible conclusion to their little tête-à-tête, that apparently harmless flirtation they had just begun. It seemed as though he had suddenly gained an almost supernatural power over her. When she lay back down in bed after her fit she had looked again like a person in a trance, she had once again assumed that sleepwalker-like expression I knew so well.

While I'd had the impression earlier that Liljan was more relaxed in Bugge's presence, now I had been witness to the exact opposite: he had caused her to have a hysterical outburst. And it had been a very definite type of outburst: it seemed like a revolt, a desperate attempt to escape his influence. But she hadn't succeeded; she had capitulated, and he had maintained control.

Over the years I've seen many peculiar types of love-making, but nothing like this. Kai Bugge – Liljan Werner? What sort of connection was there between them?

This wasn't just an ordinary summer flirtation that had begun a couple of hours ago; this was something else, something that went considerably deeper. It was clear to me that the relationship must have been going on a long time, I just hadn't noticed the little details that would have given it away. Thinking about it now, I recalled episodes from several weeks earlier – several months, for that matter – which must have pointed in this direction. Good lord, how blind I had been . . .

I was convinced of one thing, anyway: there was something obscene here somewhere, something abnormal and sinister. What had she yelled at him? Hadn't she accused him of wanting to drown her? She had seemed totally possessed when she screamed those words.

As I walked along the road, struggling in vain to find meaning in the chaos, it struck me that I'd known Bugge for over ten years. But did I really *know* him? Wasn't it possible he had a secret, a hidden side to his personality, something I'd never noticed? Maybe there was an underworld within him too, a Hades that couldn't bear the light of day? Do we really know a person just because we've drunk a few hundred highballs with them?

That was the question which, for the moment, I was unable to answer.

CHAPTER NINE

In which a revenant makes an appearance

WHEN I GOT BACK to the cabin a little later, Bugge was sitting alone by the fire, studying a thick book. He looked up and smiled cheerfully when I came in. There was nothing of the strange and frightening impression he had given me a couple of minutes ago; on the contrary, it was the old Bugge sitting there. He was just as friendly and good-natured, in his ironic way, as he usually was towards me.

'Hello,' he said. 'Welcome back. You'll have to excuse me for running you off just now.'

'Where's Liljan?' I asked. I was determined to hold the knife to his throat.

'She's asleep.' He nodded in the direction of her room.

'Just answer one question for me, Bugge.' I looked him straight in the eyes. 'What's really going on between you and Liljan?'

If I had expected him to look away evasively, I was in for a letdown. He eyed me with an almost impudent look.

'I'm just conducting a bit of field research,' he said, a little offhand. 'By the way,' he put the book down, 'there's something I'd like to ask you.'

'Go ahead.'

'You noticed Liljan's facial expression when she was walking in her sleep last night, didn't you?'

'Yes, of course.'

'And it took you a long time to wake her up?'

'About a minute.'

'To come to the point: do you have the impression she was *hypnotized*?'

I held my breath for a moment when he mentioned that word. Only now did I realize what I had been a witness to earlier: it was a hypnosis session, he had hypnotized her to sleep. 'Yes, now that you say it,' I muttered. 'I admit I've never seen a hypnotized person before, but I imagine that's how it would look.'

I tried to picture how she had looked walking along the road.

'There's one thing in particular that confirms it,' I continued. 'She seemed so willful, so determined, when she was walking towards the lake. But I had the impression that it was actually *someone else's* will being exerted on her. It was like she herself wasn't the driving force.'

Bugge nodded thoughtfully.

'Outstanding,' he said. 'Not bad at all. You're making progress, Bernhard, you're beginning to *see*.'

There was something weighing on my mind. I had to voice my suspicion.

'But if it's a case of hypnosis, then there must also be a hypnotist,' I said emphatically. 'If we're not dealing with supernatural forces, then we have to assume there's a living person behind it.'

'Agreed. An extremely logical conclusion.'

'Just between you and me, isn't it rather striking that we actually have a professional hypnotist here? Namely *you*.'

Bugge looked at me blankly for a few seconds. Then he broke into a fit of laughter.

'You suspect *me*?' he exclaimed. 'Really quite funny. I must admit that it looks bad for me. I certainly have dealt a lot with hypnosis in my treatment of acute neuroses, therefore it goes without saying that it's *me* who – I must say, you have a lot of faith in your old friends.'

I didn't like it. His cheerfulness seemed a trifle forced to me.

'But you're a bad crime writer, Bernhard. Haven't you learned by now that the culprit is always the *least* likely person? It's always a nondescript butler or a friendly old servant who commits the murders in books. It's never the man found standing over the corpse with a smoking gun in his hand.'

'I haven't said anything about murder,' I objected, a little hurt by his tone. 'We can't just assume Werner was murdered, and Liljan is still on this side of the grave – for now.'

'*For now?* That has an ominous ring to it.'

'Yes it does. To be perfectly frank, I believe that at this moment Liljan's life hangs by a thread – and an unusually thin thread at that. To put it simply, I think she's in mortal danger.'

Bugge had suddenly grown surprisingly serious.

'So you've suspected murder is afoot as well,' he said. 'And for once I think you're on the right track.'

'Are *you* starting to share Gran's view too?'

'As a matter of principle, I never share anyone else's views. I prefer to have my own opinions. But I will concede that Gran may have caught a whiff of the truth.'

'Do you really think there's someone – one of us, for example – who might have a reason for murdering Werner – and Liljan? *Two* murders. It's all totally beyond me. And that business with the lake – what's it all mean? This whole thing is a big, incoherent nightmare.'

Bugge set his book aside and leaned back in the chair.

'On the contrary. This whole thing is a *coherent* nightmare. There's a logic in what's happening, and I'm slowly starting to make out the thread running through it. After what's happened over the past twenty-four hours, I almost think I understand what's going on.'

He stopped and glanced absently out the window with

an unreadable expression. He clearly had no intention of initiating me into the mysteries of his wisdom. My friend has an irritatingly self-satisfied look at times like this. Sometimes he reminds me of a little boy who shows off a big bag of candy to his friends and brags about all the fabulous things inside, but then refuses to open it up and share the contents. I knew there was no point in asking him straight out, but I felt the itch of curiosity; I would use the indirect method and at least clear up a few details.

'You claim that Liljan was hypnotized,' I began. 'But how can that be? She's been with us the whole time, after all, and clearly nothing like that happened while we were watching. Or is it possible someone hypnotized her beforehand?'

Bugge chewed on the question for a while. Then he lit a cigarette and took several long, deep puffs.

'She was obviously hypnotized when we weren't watching over her. For example last night – just before she walked to the lake. While the rest of us were sleeping.'

'But it so happened I wasn't sleeping – thank God. And I know there was nobody else in her room. You know the walls are paper-thin in this house. I couldn't have helped hearing if someone had gone into her room and started talking with her.'

My friend shrugged his shoulders.

'Bernhard, I'm afraid your idea of hypnosis comes from reading about Olga Barcowa, the green-eyed adventuress.* It's a popular misconception that hypnosis is done with the *eyes*, that the hypnotist must be in the same room with the subject, in other words. But it's not at all necessary for them to be in the same room in order to make contact. The *voice* is the main thing. I once conducted a very successful hypnosis session by telephone.'

'But I can assure you I didn't hear any voices, either inside or outside the house. It was totally silent. And what you said about the telephone doesn't apply in this case – it's not as though the murderer could have called here long distance from Oslo, for instance. I really don't see where you're going with this.'

'When I say *voice*, I don't necessarily mean the physio-logical voice, sound impressions received by the eardrum. There's also such a thing as a mental voice that can be used to contact other people – wirelessly, you might say. The mental voice can also be turned into an organ of a person's will, if you understand what I mean.'

'No, God knows I don't.'

'Then I'll try to explain. You've surely heard of some-thing called magic. Or haven't you?'

'I did finish middle school, you know.'

'I should hope so. Most people consider magic to be a useless old superstition, silly nonsense practiced by people in the olden days, long before Newton and Einstein brought us around to a more enlightened way of thinking. And yet we're subject to magical effects and mysterious emanations from other people more often than we suspect. We're still living in the age of magic, and we often practice both white and black magic without knowing it . . .'

Bugge blew some thick, oval-shaped smoke rings towards the bookshelf.

'*Intentional* magic isn't dead either. A few years ago I was talking to a woman from Finnmark. She told me at least one in five people there can still cast spells and practice sorcery. Even she knew the art, and she confided to me that if she wanted to, she could put a spell on me any time she wished and force me to come to her at night. Fortunately she was tactful enough not to make use of it. She wasn't my type.'

'Why bring all this up?'

'Because it's tied in with our topic. Magic isn't super-natural in and of itself; it's a phenomenon closely related to hypnosis. It's – how should I put it – a kind of *remote hypnosis*. You're probably thinking I've lost my mind, but I'm convinced that Liljan is a victim of black magic, pure and simple. Somebody somewhere has put a spell on her. Werner was the first victim, and now she's the one in the danger zone.'

'That's pure hocus pocus. I thought you were a psychoanalyst, not a witch doctor. You don't mean you really *believe* in that kind of thing?'

'It's not a question of belief. I *know* it's the case.'

'If only Mørk could hear this. He'd be thrilled to have a disciple like you . . .'

Our conversation was interrupted when Sonja opened the door and came into the room. She was panting and red-faced from running. But her cheeks weren't flushed solely from the physical exertion; her face was lit up with an expression of exaltation and inner excitement. She walked straight up to me and grabbed my arm.

'You have to come to the woods right away,' she said, her agitation making it a little hard for her to speak. 'Gran has discovered something – well, something very strange – '

We followed her. A few hundred yards into the woods we met Gran and Mørk, who were busy doing something rather peculiar. They were both on their knees, evidently examining the ground. Gran looked up as we approached and cast a slightly grouchy sidelong glance at Bugge. He didn't seem to be in a particularly good mood, but Mørk on the other hand had a expression of satisfaction and triumph. Sonja tugged on my arm.

'Look there,' she said, pointing down.

I followed the direction of her index finger without understanding at first what she meant. Then it suddenly dawned on me, and I felt an involuntary shudder run through me.

What Gran and Mørk were examining was a bare strip

of soft soil, in which footprints could clearly be seen. But it was the impression of only one foot, the left one. Where the tracks of the right foot should have been, there were only circular indentations, two inches in diameter. They were the marks left by a wooden leg.

I immediately thought of what Sheriff Bråten had told us the first evening, that people down in the village had often seen Tore Gruvik's footprints in the woods. I hadn't attached much importance to it then; I had assumed it was just a popular embellishment of the old legend. But now I had seen it with my own eyes. At least now we had established that we were no longer alone there in the woods.

Mørk got up and looked at Bugge and Gran with provoking irony.

'Well, gentlemen?' he said, brushing the dirt off his clothes. 'How do we explain this? After all, there's a natural explanation for everything, right?'

Gran grumbled something and stood up as well. I looked at Bugge. His face was totally calm, not a muscle twitched. He didn't appear particularly shocked by this discovery. But he was clearly interested. He stood examining the footprints with that characteristic squinting look of his.

'Funny,' he muttered. 'It all fits together perfectly. Just perfectly.'

'Couldn't we follow these tracks and find out where they lead?' Gran asked. 'Or can't you figure out where they come from?'

'I'm afraid not. It would be hard to follow them across the heath, and judging from the look of it, they lead towards the path, where the soil has been trodden down hard. It seems this revenant likes being near our cabin; the direction of the footprints shows that he took a walk over that way. As far as I can tell, these footprints are from last night.'

Last night! So that creature had been close by the house

when Liljan walked to the lake in a trance. He had followed her with his eyes as she walked – or perhaps it was *his* eyes that had driven her there? He had stood like an invisible pillar in the darkness when I ran out to stop her – maybe I had passed within only a few yards of him? When I thought back on it, I knew I had felt it. I had sensed that gaze, those dead, hateful eyes staring at me through the trees . . .

I felt Sonja's strong little fingers gripping my arm so hard that it almost hurt. I took her hand and gave it an encouraging little squeeze. It's always a comfort to have someone weaker to protect when you're not feeling particularly brave yourself.

The air grew more and more oppressive as the afternoon went on. The insects settled down sleepily and listlessly on the windowpanes; even the flies, normally so lively and temperamental, had completely lost their spark of life. They dragged themselves wearily around the window screen and let themselves be put out of their misery without even offering any resistance. There was an intense sultriness in the air, a stored-up electrical tension demanding release.

It might have been 9:30 or 10 p.m. and it had gotten fairly dark outside, when the chef – my wife – decided I had to go and fetch her a couple of buckets of water.

I think I made one or two objections before obeying her order. I've always been an obedient soldier in my marriage and only resist an order from high command when it involves a direct attack on my comfort, and then only reluctantly. And it occurred to me that was the case now. But after some vain attempts to negotiate, during which my wife finally threatened to ask someone else to go, I wound up giving in, took a bucket in each hand and set out.

It was quite a hike. I had to go all the way down to the

river to get the water, and to be honest, I wasn't particularly keen on a lonely nighttime stroll – especially after the discovery we had made that morning. I could have asked Bugge or one of the others to go with me, of course, but for some reason I decided to go alone. Maybe I wanted to put my nerves to the test.

I whistled a popular tune and tried to cheer myself up as best I could as I strolled through the woods with the two water buckets swinging in my hands. I was bound and determined to conquer my old weakness, my fear of the woods; I wouldn't let myself be frightened by my overactive imagination. I armored myself with a nonchalant attitude, making it a point of honor to walk as slowly and leisurely as possible. Wasn't it the twentieth century, after all?

I reached the river without incident, filled the buckets, and started the trek back. During those few minutes night had fallen. The last glimmer of sunshine in the western sky had gone out, and now the moon hung like an enormous carnival spotlight above the trees, sending a sickly white light over the landscape. Something feverish had come over nature itself. The muggy air lay over the trees like a blanket; the wind, coming from the woods in small, hot gusts, resembled a gasping breath, like the respiration of a sick person. To the south a woolly mass of bluish-black storm clouds rose slowly above the horizon. They came closer every minute; now and then the silent lightning flickered through the darkness – heat lightning. The storm would reach us within the hour.

I was fairly exhausted by the time I made it back to the road. It had been a strenuous march, and the heavy air hadn't helped. I was sweating like a pig and had to set the buckets down and take a little break. I pulled a cigarette stump from my pocket and took several deep, refreshing puffs.

As I stood there resting, a strange notion suddenly came

to me. Thinking back on it, I can't just write it off as a random whim, a hunch; there was something else at work. I suddenly had an irresistible urge to walk towards the lake!

I think at that moment I must have been in a kind of dissociative state; it was like I didn't really have control over myself. Maybe the hike with the buckets was to blame. After all, I'm not used to that sort of physical exertion, and my friend Mørk claims that any use of the body beyond what is strictly necessary is a danger to a person's conscious state. All I know is that I started to move towards Blue Lake on some kind of impulse; my legs carried me away mechanically, something was drawing me there. I was almost a little surprised when I found myself standing at the shore of the lake a minute later. I was instantly awake again and couldn't really account for why I had made that detour.

Yet at that time of night the lake was a breathtaking sight; it seemed even more magical than by day. The dark tree stumps looked as though made of flesh and blood in that light – large, deformed heads emerging from the depths, with dripping green hair hanging down over shining eyes; it was like something out of one of Kittelsen's paintings.* The lilies had taken on a feverish glow, a frenzied whiteness in the moonlight. They were almost like living animals, standing out in sharp contrast to the lake's dead, bluish-black surface. The surrounding trees were also alive, a dense crowd of humanlike creatures. The green darkness of the woods concealed strange faces, and the branches moved imperceptibly in the wind like fumbling arms. The croaking of the frogs could be heard on all sides. It sounded like it was coming from the depths of an abyss.

As I stood looking out over the lake, I felt the old sense of fear sneaking up on me, the indefinable feeling that something was threatening me. But I was powerless to move from the spot, something was holding me back. My head was clear, I was totally conscious, but my consciousness was captured in some way, magnetically drawn to this spot. A thought occurred to me: this was something like what Werner had experienced and described. But I knew that I would keep control over myself the whole time; *I* wouldn't yield to some mad impulse.

I stood silently on the shore, staring down into the water. Why? I felt an indescribable urge to try what Werner had called his 'great experiment'. I knew if I went on standing there I would see something extraordinary, I would experience something fantastic . . .

And after what happened the next few seconds, I had no reason to feel disappointed.

There was a sound from the opposite shore, thirty or forty yards away, which made me suddenly look up. Something was moving through the thicket, a twig had snapped. I directed my gaze towards the spot from which the sound had come – and immediately felt a tingling chill run down my spine, like a thousand tiny icicles pricking my skin. I strained my eyes. Could my vision have deceived me? Was it an optical illusion? No, I could see quite plainly: on the other side of the lake a figure stood watching me.

It was a man. He stood totally motionless between the trees, the contours of his body clearly outlined against the moonlit background. But if it hadn't been for that little noise, I wouldn't have noticed him; I would have taken that figure to be a shadow, a random shape in the darkness. I stared at him, mesmerized, maybe for several minutes. My eyes burned, my temples pounded; the feeling of chill had spread all the way to my fingertips.

I knew with instinctive certainty that the being across from me was no living person. It was a dead man, a revenant. The figure was not tangible; it seemed to me that it was slowly fading, slipping into something misty, indefinable. I couldn't make out his face clearly, but I could feel his *eyes* fixed on me the whole time. They shone with an ice-cold flame, a smoldering, hateful glow; they expressed a willpower the likes of which I had never felt before. It was a gaze that was not of this world.

I don't know how long I stood there staring before I screamed. A low little cry, an inarticulate groan; it was as though the fear suddenly trickled out of my mouth. As if on signal, the figure made a half turn, hobbled into the forest, and disappeared. I say *hobbled*: he dragged one foot behind him – it was an artificial foot, a wooden leg . . .

I made my way home, my limbs quivering. My entire body was bathed in a cold sweat, and shapes flickered before my eyes. It was all I could do to carry the buckets.

'You were gone a long time,' my wife said, looking me up and down when I had finally set the buckets down in the kitchen and taken a deep breath.

'You should be happy it wasn't longer,' I muttered.

I didn't say anything to the others about what I had seen. I didn't want them thinking me even more foolish than I really am.

CHAPTER TEN

In which Mørk thinks enough is enough,
while Bugge is insatiable

THE STORM BROKE OUT at exactly 10:30 p.m.

The black clouds moved slowly but surely across the sky, like an invincible motorized army. Little by little they conquered the entire heavens; the moon was captured and annihilated, and an Egyptian darkness descended over the landscape. The distant rumbling came closer and closer: Heaven's artillery was approaching. The white flashes flickered at short intervals and with increasing strength, and the cannons above us fired methodically towards our positions. Finally they had pinpointed their target; the first lightning crackled over the forest like a tremendous spear of fire, a howling projectile of flames. It was followed by a violent bang, a booming detonation. It was like the sound of two massive planets colliding in the night. Sonja carefully closed all the windows.

We all sat huddled together, attacking the last of Gran's aquavit. Personally, I've always thought there's something cozy about thunderstorms, something intimate and atmospheric. People are brought closer together in a way when the forces of nature rage; what's more, women's fragility is so charmingly exposed every time it thunders. But in this situation it was just harrowing, like further wear on my nerves. Among other things, I knew the house didn't have a lightning rod. I was still nervous and ill at ease after my little experience in the woods, and even the golden, intoxicating liquid in my glass couldn't help me with that.

Gran looked to be in a similarly foul mood. For the past twenty-four hours he hadn't been himself, and I was fully aware it was because of Liljan. All day long she'd hung around Bugge, especially after the peculiar episode that morning, an episode for which I still hadn't gotten any explanation; Bugge consistently evaded all my questions. I was left to my own imagination, but to be honest, I was in no condition to come up with an explanation. I felt confused and depressed – and with good reason. This sort of thing had never happened to me before: a series of strange events suddenly starting to occur around me without my being able to make any sense of it whatsoever.

For a moment – after the scene in Liljan's room – I'd had a vague suspicion of Bugge, but I had let that drop after talking with him. He seemed so reassuringly confident and even-keeled, and *what* could I suspect him of, anyway? Black magic? He must have been kidding with me when he mentioned all that about magic. Or maybe it was just a smokescreen to hide his real thoughts and intentions. In any case, that word 'magic' had stuck in my mind. There were ghosts and witchcraft in the air in this place; all of us were *different* from being here. I was even getting the feeling I might go crazy if I stayed in that atmosphere much longer.

Bugge always addressed himself to Liljan when he spoke – not just with his voice, but with his body, his will, his whole personality. My impression from earlier was confirmed: he had a stimulating, strengthening effect on her; she talked and laughed and felt safe in his presence. Electric currents ran between the two of them, something radiated out from him to her. There could be no doubt that Gran was the odd man out.

How could that be reconciled with her fantastic outburst that morning, when in a wild frenzy she had flung herself at Bugge, screaming that he wanted to drown her? Was it just hysteria, a nervous aftereffect of what she had experienced the night before? Possibly. But why had she gone to the lake, why had she gotten such a shock? I couldn't answer that, I couldn't answer anything. I realized quite clearly that my understanding of human psychology must be dangerously close to zero.

Mørk had gotten comfortable in his chair and was watching the burning logs in the fireplace. The flames cast flickering shadows on his pale, defined features. The room around us lay in darkness.

'There's something curious about *horror*,' he said. 'Most people have felt it. In reality, the feeling of horror is the expression of something quite definite.'

He paused for effect, folded his hands over his stomach, and leaned his head against the chair back. In that light, his face looked like it had been modeled out of plaster. It looked like a death mask.

'In a country like India, people interact with the dead every single day, see ghosts every day in the most literal sense – without feeling the slightest hint of horror. And why? Because Eastern people – especially Indians – have a very different spiritual culture from us Europeans. We think we've found the ultimate truths, the immortal wisdom, and in reality we're totally ignorant; we're children, no wiser spiritually than primitive forest dwellers. The only things we've managed to produce are some technological toys whose proper place is in the nursery. You can see our impotence most clearly in our fear of the spirit world, our terror of ghosts – we're so frightened out of our wits that we deny their existence. But an Indian doesn't feel any such fear. Through mental practice and meditation he has made himself comfortable with the unseen world; he is *initiated*. It's as natural for him to talk to spirits as it is for us to brush our teeth, slander our neighbors, and write bad literature.'

I noticed that Bugge had assumed the ironic smile he always has ready for such occasions. For some reason, he's incapable of taking his friend seriously. Personally, I found what Mørk was saying quite compelling. As far as I was concerned, it was all very relevant – apart from that bit about the bad literature.

'Galileo's judges refused to look through his telescope,' Mørk continued. 'And why? Because it would have destroyed their worldview – it would have blasted away the foundation underneath them, it might have driven them mad. They felt *horror*. For the same reason, a modern Westerner is scared of seeing a demon or meeting a ghost. His worldview would instantly explode. The whole impressive, naive construction of steel and concrete, chemical formulas and sex literature, psychoanalysis and cultural snobbery – all of it would collapse like a house of cards. He doesn't *dare* see the spiritual world, he doesn't *dare* look into the dangerous telescope, he doesn't *dare* leave the nursery. He feels a chilling horror at the very thought of it . . .'

A resounding boom interrupted Mørk's observations.

'It struck somewhere close by!' Sonja exclaimed. We went over to the window.

The storm had increased in size and strength over the past few minutes. Lightning ripped through the darkness continually, spreading colossal fans of fire across the sky, embroideries of flame that stood silently in space for fractions of a second. The thunder rolled incessantly, an avalanche of noise; it sounded as though the universe were coming apart at the seams. The rain had set in too – and what rain! It came down in heavy hammer blows against the windows, foaming against the glass; one breaker wave after another swept in over the garden walls, and I could hear water dripping through the roof in places. Every time lightning lit up the landscape, it flashed green in the puddles; I had the sensation of being in a huge aquarium or at the bottom of the sea, where the trees were underwater forests and the lightning was phosphorescent sea life.

'A hell of a storm,' Gran muttered. 'I've never seen anything like it in these latitudes.'

'It struck again over there!' Sonja grabbed my arm.

A gigantic flaming sword had pierced straight down into the ground thirty or forty yards away. A tree was splintered like a twig, its top falling to the ground in flames. There was a gust of wind so violent that we could feel it even through the wall and the window. I held my breath for several seconds while the tremendous boom tore through my ears.

'Thanks for bringing it to my attention,' I said with affectionate irony. 'Another lightning strike like that and we won't have to dread a long and painful old age.'

I was trying to keep things light, but I didn't feel particularly light-hearted. Sonja pressed up close to me.

'I wonder if there's anyone out tonight,' she whispered. 'Here in the woods.'

'What makes you think such a thing?'

'I don't *think* it. I said, I wonder – '

These words touched something deep inside me; once again I felt the little tingling sensation at my scalp. After all, I *knew* there was someone outside – I had seen him myself!

There was a strange, doubly dreadful atmosphere that night. Out there in the darkness *two* dangers lay in wait for us. First there was the purely physical menace of the thunderstorm, and then there was another threat of a strange, unfathomable nature. The dark woods concealed a monster, a creature that hated us, an unseen, destructive force. Sooner or later he would strike, quickly and crushingly, like lightning shattering a tree trunk. In the furious forces of nature there was a symbolic warning, the warning that another storm would soon break over us; the air had long been heavy with it . . .

'I don't like watching the lightning,' said Liljan. She was

standing with one hand on Bugge's arm, as Gran observed them from off to the side. 'The more we watch it, the worse it gets. Can't we just sit down and pretend nothing's happening?'

We went back to our places and sat down. Gran poured out a round with the last of the liquor. Bugge took a sip from his glass and turned to Mørk.

'Your analysis of horror is quite interesting,' he said. 'Apart from being completely wrong, which is of course a petty and narrow-minded objection. The feeling of horror has nothing to do with an external spirit world; it comes from an inner, repressed world inside us. When a person is scared of ghosts, deep down it's himself he's afraid of. He fears his own specter, that unconscious, dead part of himself that suddenly takes on new and sinister life at night. He is afraid of the dark because the dark calls to the night side of his nature: the destroyer, the murderer, the predator – everything that the civilized part of him has conquered. There are no other ghosts.'

Mørk shook his head in irritation.

'You deny the existence of the supernatural world because you haven't seen it,' he declared. 'And in doing so you – in a spiritual sense – place yourself on the same footing as the Bantu who denies the existence of ice.'

'Let's change the subject,' I interjected. 'Isn't there anything more pleasant to talk about?'

I didn't like that conversation anymore. It came far too close to what had been worrying me and what I had been trying in vain to stop thinking about; it made the already macabre atmosphere even gloomier. When Mørk and Bugge ignored me, however, and went on with their discussion, I decided to go and get a good book from my room. I got up from my chair and walked resolutely towards the door.

'Get me a pillow while you're at it!' Sonja called after me.

Our bedroom was, as I've previously mentioned, fairly isolated: you had to go through the kitchen to get there; there was no way in from any other room. The kitchen was extremely dark; it was like walking into a catacomb. I had left my lighter behind in the living room and had to fumble my way carefully across the floor to reach the door to the bedroom. The storm outside had taken a short pause, and the rain had lost its explosive power; the violent Niagara rumbling had dissolved into a gentler tone, a steady rinsing sound. It was relatively quiet for a few seconds, and that silence enabled me to pick up a faint noise that would otherwise have been drowned out in the racket. I was just about to grab the door handle when I suddenly stopped and pricked up my ears. I stood as quiet as a mouse and listened. Was it my imagination?

At first I was sure I must have heard wrong, or rather, I must have interpreted the sound wrong. There was no question I had really heard something, but it could have been the usual creaking and scratching in the walls. There are so many odd sounds in an old house like that one, and it's easy to mistake them for something else. Especially when you're jumpy and overly sensitive to such things.

But then it came again, and this time there could be no doubt: the sound was coming from inside the bedroom. And it wasn't a dead sound; it wasn't the normal, melancholy groans of the rotting walls. Something living was moving in there – there were *footsteps* on the floorboards. Someone was in our room!

In a situation like this, a rational person says to himself, 'Good lord, it's only rats. There's no reason to be scared, there's no such thing as ghosts.' Rats are reliable: they turn out to be the explanation for ninety percent of apparently supernatural phenomena; the other ten percent can be attributed to mice. But I knew that neither rats nor mice had caused the noises in there. I could clearly hear a floorboard creaking under a heavy foot. They were definitely human footsteps.

I stood there in total uncertainty for almost a whole minute. My body felt paralyzed and numb, my knees were weak, and my heart pounded as if in the advanced stages of nicotine poisoning. What I wanted most of all, of course, was to make a quick about-face and return to the others. But I knew I'd be laughed at if I went in with bulging eyes and trembling hands and told them there was a ghost in my room. I'd run the risk that we wouldn't find anything when we all went together to investigate.

The creature on the other side of the door had been silent for several moments. I guessed that he must be somewhere in the middle of the room, by the foot of my bed. I thought I heard him breathing – strong, laborious breaths, a rhythmic, wheezing sound. Had he heard me? Was he standing there motionless in the darkness, waiting for me to open the door?

I heard steps again. They moved cautiously towards one of the walls, the one adjoining Liljan's room. This time I perceived something new: the steps made different sounds, depending on which foot was touching the floor. Every second step sounded like a blunt object made of wood or cork striking the floor. It had a *limping* rhythm.

At that moment I pulled myself together. Or maybe it was just a wild impulse, giving in to my burning curiosity. There are times in your life when you suddenly cast all inhibitions aside and take a *leap*, without self-control or deliberation. There's a certain thrilling pleasure in surprising yourself and overcoming your petty, cowardly concerns. I wanted to see what was hiding behind that door.

It was done in a second. I gritted my teeth, clenched my right hand into a fist, ready to defend myself against whatever might be in there, and pressed the handle down quickly with my left. Then I pushed the door open.

Just then lightning struck. At precisely the same fraction of a second as my foot touched the threshold, a flood of chalk-white light came through the window. It was as if a magnesium bomb had exploded right in my face.

The thunder came a moment after, rolling over the house in a gigantic wave. The walls quivered like during an earthquake.

I was totally blinded. For as long as the lightning lasted, it was impossible to discern anything in there; everything was equally white. Ceiling and walls and beds and table all merged together – and in the next instant everything around me went totally black. I was as blind as a bat. Strange figures danced before my eyes; I stood there blinking helplessly at the impenetrable darkness. My head felt like I'd just received a well-aimed blow to the jaw.

I stood there for a few seconds trying to collect myself, but my eyes didn't have time to get used to the darkness. I was struck with panic; I had the sensation that two hands were reaching out for me, grasping for my clothes, trying to grab me. He, the other, came closer, took a step towards me . . . I turned on my heels at top speed and raced out of the room.

In the kitchen I knocked my forehead against the wall and was on the verge of passing out; a storm of stars whizzed past my eyes. I was completely beside myself with terror, flailing my arms around as I tried to find the exit. I stumbled over the doorstep leading to the hall and toppled forward, but got to my feet again and reached the door to the living room. I threw it open and stumbled inside. The others stared at me with an expression of unfeigned astonishment.

'There's someone in there,' I stammered. 'There's someone in that room – '

If it had been my intention to frighten them, I would have had good reason to be pleased with the result. It was obvious I wasn't the only one on edge; they shot up from their seats as though I'd cried 'Fire!' Only Bugge remained sitting calmly.

'What are you saying?' Sonja exclaimed.

'That there's someone in our bedroom,' I repeated. 'Go and look for yourselves, you'll see.'

'*Who* is in there?' Gran grabbed my arm hard.

'No idea. Unfortunately we didn't get the chance to introduce ourselves. Besides, I didn't have my lighter with me. Take the paraffin lamp.'

'Are you totally sure it wasn't just your imagination?'

'Positive. Go and look for yourself, damn it.'

'Why not?' Bugge got up from his chair. 'A nocturnal guest looking for shelter here in this awful weather isn't so unthinkable, after all. Let's go and give him a hearty welcome. You have a flashlight, don't you, Harald?'

Gran nodded and drew a small, nickel-plated, cylinder-shaped flashlight from his pocket. He switched it on and went into the hall, the rest of us following him, a couple of us a little hesitantly. Personally I made sure to be at the back of the line.

In the kitchen we stopped; that is, it was our leader Gran who came to a halt. The bright, cone-shaped beam cut through the darkness, revealing that the door in front of us was ajar – I hadn't closed it behind me during my hasty retreat. The thunder was still rolling outside, but it had already gotten noticeably weaker. The storm was no longer right over our heads, it was moving on. No sound came from the room, at least nothing that could be heard over the monotonous, whipping stream of rain against the windowpanes. It was as though something compelled us to stop in front of that door. A cold rush of air flowed out through the narrow gap. Clearly none of us wanted to be the first to go in.

'Well?' Bugge said, giving Gran a little push. 'Is there any reason to stop here? Or should I take the flashlight?'

Gran manned up, pushed the door open with his foot, and took a determined step over the threshold. We followed him in a tight column. Only then did I notice that the window was open; Sonja must have forgotten to close it. It swung back and forth in the wind, and a fine shower of rain sprayed onto the floor. Gran moved the flashlight beam systematically over every square inch of the room. I held my breath tensely the whole time.

'Empty,' he declared at last. 'There's no one here. You must have been seeing things after all, Bernhard.'

'But I assure you there was a man in here,' I said. 'My five senses are still intact, after all.'

'Did you see him?'

'No, but I heard him. I was standing maybe a yard away from him and heard that he was there. There was no chance of a mistake – '.

Bugge struck a match and lit a candle on the nightstand, while Sonja went over and closed the window.

'Don't step in that water!' Gran exclaimed suddenly. 'Stand aside, Sonja.'

Once again he let the flashlight beam glide searchingly across the floor, and now he stopped at a point just in front of the window. He bent down and examined some wet spots.

'Damn,' he muttered. 'I didn't see this before.'

I bent down too and saw what he was looking at. What I had at first taken for some puddles of rainwater turned out to be mud. There was a series of similar spots all over the floor. And they weren't ordinary, irregular mud puddles. They had a quite definite shape; they were prints left by a human foot. To the right of these tracks – running parallel at a distance of about eight inches – ran a series of smaller spots, impressions left by a wooden leg. They were a perfect match for the tracks we had found in the woods that morning.

'So *he* was our visitor,' said Bugge. 'It seems to me that our occult friend is starting to get a little intrusive.'

Gran was examining the windowsill. There were some mud stains there too.

'He came in through the window,' he concluded. 'And went out the same way. Here are two prints left by his shoe.'

He shined the light on them; they had almost been washed away by the rain. One footprint pointed in towards the room, the other faced outside. The latter was the clearest, evidently because it had been made later.

'This is starting to get dangerous,' said a voice from the back of the room. It was Mørk. He had been silent a while; now he stood with his arms crossed, considering the footprints with a grim expression.

'Dangerous?' Bugge gave him an inquisitive look.

'Yes, precisely – dangerous. Haven't you finally opened your eyes to what sort of powers we're dealing with? If so, then this expedition hasn't been a total waste of time and should now be considered at an end. Hopefully you don't require further proof of the existence of the supernatural. I suggest we return to town at once.'

I was grateful to him for finally putting into words what I had been reluctant to say the entire time. I longed to get away from there. The thought of staying another day was almost unbearable. But Bugge immediately dashed my hopes.

'Not a chance,' said Bugge. 'Why should we return home with the case still totally unresolved? Didn't we come here to clear up Werner's death? There's no reason to run away helter skelter just because it's a little spooky here; that only makes the whole thing more interesting. To tell the truth, I'm liking it better and better up here. I think this is a very entertaining house.'

'Rubbish,' said Mørk. His cheeks were aflame and he

seemed agitated. 'How long is this game to go on? Maybe you think we can treat it all as some sort of parlor game? Don't you know it's dangerous to fool around with the supernatural world? I guarantee that if we don't get out of here immediately, a catastrophe will occur before we know it.'

'*I* for one am staying,' Bugge declared firmly. 'I've taken on a problem, and I have no intention of leaving this place until I've solved it. I don't like to quit halfway through. I'm afraid it's one of my principles, just about the only one. But if anyone is set on turning back, now's the time to do it.'

'Of course we're staying,' said Gran. For the past thirty seconds he had stood bent over the window, examining something outside in the darkness by the glow of his flashlight. He too seemed excited; when he turned towards the rest of us again, his eyes had a strangely frenzied glint. 'There's no reason to give up now, just when we're on the right track. In fact tonight I think I'm beginning to see how it all fits together.'

There was a short, tense pause after that remark. There was nothing more to say.

'Maybe one of the ladies feels like leaving?' Bugge suggested. 'What about you, Sonja?'

My wife shook her head.

'I don't want to go,' she said. 'I think this is getting more and more exciting.'

'And you, Liljan?'

He looked searchingly into her eyes. She answered his gaze with a peculiar, submissive look, staring at him almost like a dog looks at its master.

'I'm not going anywhere until I find out what happened to Bjørn.' Her voice sounded firm.

Mørk shrugged in resignation. 'Very well,' he said. 'As you wish. We'll stay here, by all means. People do have a weakness for building their towns on the edge of volcanoes, after all. But let the record show that I warned you, and I accept no responsibility for whatever may happen . . .'

The storm passed further away. The roll of the thunder grew weaker and weaker, like the sound of a large vehicle passing by, and the lightning flickered only occasionally in the darkness. The rain had become a quiet trickle, a delicate violin tone in the night. The fresh, cool scent of wet trees streamed in through the window. Nature seemed to have been set free again after the storm.

We went back to the living room, Bugge and I bringing up the rear. My friend gave me a smiling, sidelong glance.

'Good lord, you're as pale as a corpse, Bernhard,' he said. 'And your hands are shaking. Do you want a cigarette?'

I took it and inhaled several greedy puffs. The mild, fragrant smoke flowed soothingly down into my body.

'What do you think about the latest developments?' I asked.

He stared absently into space.

'It's rather curious,' he said. 'The man with the wooden leg – it sounds like the title of a bad crime novel. But I don't think this crime novel is going to be so bad. There are still a couple of pretty dramatic chapters left, and to be honest I'm really looking forward to reading them . . .'

CHAPTER ELEVEN

In which catastrophe strikes

I DIDN'T FIND GOING TO BED in my room particularly tempting that night, especially considering I was all alone in there. My wife insisted on sleeping in Liljan's room; she wanted to look after her, in case there was a repeat of the previous night's sleepwalking scene. I lay on my bed for a long time without taking off my clothes. I tried to read a book by the glow of the paraffin lamp, but I had a hard time focusing on my reading; the day's events kept running through my mind and the letters skipped meaninglessly before my eyes. Every so often I glanced towards the window as if I expected to see someone suddenly pop up there, but it was impossible to discern anything through the dark panes; it was like staring into a black cave. The only sound in the silence was the water trickling down the glass.

It was a relief when Bugge came in fifteen minutes later in dressing gown and pajamas. He had a large book under his arm.

'Hello,' he said. 'I think I'll crash in here with you tonight. Gran's in one of his moods.'

'You're most welcome,' I said warmly. 'Nice of you to keep me company. To be honest, I didn't find it too cozy sleeping in this room alone. What's the matter with Gran?'

Bugge flung himself on the other bed, resting his head on his hands.

'He's as irritable as a hysterical woman. Granted, treating hysterical women is my specialty, but everything in moderation. I prefer to sleep in peaceful surroundings.'

'Maybe he's jealous?' I suggested. 'Maybe he thinks you're trying to take Liljan from him?'

My friend ignored the question. He opened the book he had brought and started to leaf through it.

'Some light reading?'

He glanced at the cover. '*The Divine Comedy* by Dante Alighieri. Famous writer of the early Italian Renaissance. It's supposed to be a good book; it's received several positive reviews, according to the publisher's blurb.'

'I didn't think anybody but Mørk and Werner was interested in those old classics,' I said with a smile. 'That's the funny thing about classics: the less they're read, the more their reputation grows; their great secret consists in being completely unreadable. Personally I prefer John Dickson Carr and Agatha Christie.'

Bugge had pulled a small piece of loose paper from between the book's pages. He held it up to the light and considered it carefully.

'I read Dostoevsky's outstanding crime novels when I was seventeen, but sadly I haven't bothered much about literature ever since,' he said. 'And actually I'm less interested in this book than I am in the bookmark inside. It's really an unusually distinctive bookmark.'

My friend sometimes gets these eccentric moods, but this struck me as being totally uninteresting. I didn't feel the least bit curious. I'm not the sort to go nuts over a rare edition or feel my soul go into raptures at the sight of an old postage stamp. I lay silent for a while, staring at the ceiling.

'Why were you so adamant in rejecting Mørk's suggestion that we go back to the city?' I asked. 'Is there really any reason to stay? This whole trip is completely pointless. We're not accomplishing anything here.'

'On the contrary,' Bugge declared. 'We're accomplishing a great deal. As I just told you, I've come across a most extraordinary bookmark.'

'Bookmark!' I sneered in annoyance. 'That has nothing to do with anything.'

'I wouldn't say that. A bookmark can be a very significant document. Wouldn't you like to see it?'

He handed me a little sheet of paper, apparently torn out of an ordinary ruled notebook. One side was covered in shapes and numbers – the kinds of things a person often scribbles distractedly when their thoughts are elsewhere and there's a pencil and paper at hand.

I looked at it for a few seconds and gave up, shaking my head.

'What do you mean, this is a very significant document? Somebody scribbling random shapes on a sheet of paper doesn't mean anything, does it? This is just a pointless doodle. It looks like someone did it while they were delirious.'

'Precisely, my dear Bernhard. That's precisely why it's interesting. The sorts of things a person does when "delirious", as you put it, can reveal the mind's important secrets. The subconscious suddenly breaks through and takes advantage of the conscious mind's control being weakened. Little drawings like this one can tell far more about a person than he himself even realizes. You should always be careful when you're distracted and running your pencil across a page; you might be unconsciously writing your autobiography.'

'But good lord, I've often doodled on a piece of paper

while I'm working, sitting and waiting for inspiration to come. I have piles of papers like this one at home on my desk.'

'No doubt. And if a literary historian trained in psycho-analysis were to get hold of them, he would be able to write a most unpleasant thesis on what lies behind your writing.'

'I'll burn them as soon as I get home,' I muttered.

Bugge smiled. 'Look a little closer at this document,' he said. 'You can consider it as a picture puzzle with the question: Who is the murderer?'

I did as he asked, but without any worthwhile result.

'I don't think I'll win one of those prizes they give clever children,' I said. 'But as far as I can tell, the two figures are probably telephone numbers. 23 841? Isn't that Mørk's number, by the way?'

I handed the paper back to him with a questioning look. He was still smiling.

'Maybe you deserve a little consolation prize,' he said. 'But it'll have to be small . . .'

It wasn't easy for me to get to sleep that night. Long after we had put out the paraffin lamp I lay there staring into space. I still couldn't shake off the recent events; I was filled with a quivering unease. I still saw the figure at the lake before me, the stiff, frozen stare aimed straight at me, the sudden hobbling movements when he disappeared into the woods, dragging his dead foot behind him. And I relived the terrifying seconds when I stood here in the bedroom a couple of yards from him, when I felt him coming towards me, stretching out his hands . . . The images flickered through my mind like a kaleidoscope; they resembled clips from a grotesque film, the type of film that would never get past the censors.

I heard Bugge's calm, regular breathing beside me; he was sleeping soundly, smiling like a child. I was a little annoyed at his unshakable emotional balance. There's always something irritating about people who, through some freak biological coincidence, have steel wires running through their bodies instead of nerves. I wondered if he even felt pain in his teeth when the dentist drilled into them.

Finally I slept a little too. I gradually relaxed and shut out the world around me, and my controlled, waking fantasies slipped little by little into dreams. Once again I was at the lake, and again I saw Tore Gruvik standing on the opposite shore, staring at me. This time I made him out more clearly. His head was disproportionately large, and his face was no longer human. His body was naked and had a moldy green color from the waist up; it shone with a dull, slimy glow in the moonlight. His arms were unusually short and had three unjointed fingers on each hand. Only his lower body was human; he was half-frog, half-human ... He didn't move. But his eyes, his enormous, expressionless eyes, were fixed on me the whole time, emanating a mysterious power, slowly trying to trap me, to hypnotize me ...

I must have woken up from this – to put it mildly – unpleasant dream after about half an hour of sleep. In a sort of semi-conscious state I heard a door opening somewhere in the house. I sat up for a moment in bed. Was it Liljan? But then once again I heard the creaking of a door; the sound wasn't coming from Liljan's room, it was further away. Reassured, I sank back onto the pillows. A little later I caught the faint sound of shuffling steps across the living room floor. There was the metallic squeak of a door handle and the front door was pushed open. Someone was going out into the night. I had just about dozed off when these impressions came to me, and I didn't think about it at all. I simply couldn't. I was already well on my way to being asleep.

A while later I woke up again, and this time I was wide awake for a few seconds. I sat up in bed and rubbed my eyes vigorously, trying to clear my head. There was an odd ringing in my ears; I felt quite certain that I had heard a scream. A distant, piercing sound far out in the darkness, a short, terrible cry as if from a person in great danger.

'Bugge!' I whispered. 'Are you awake? Wasn't that someone screaming?'

But he didn't answer. A rhythmic snoring coming from his bed told me that he was sleeping like a rock; the noise from his nostrils was like the grinding of a mill. Good lord, what a sound sleeper!

I closed my eyes and listened. It had gone silent outside. The rain had stopped and the night wind was rustling quietly through the woods. I stayed sitting up for maybe two minutes, but nothing happened, no unusual noises stood out amid the nocturnal rustling. I relaxed. I must have dreamt I heard the scream, or maybe Bugge had whimpered in his sleep. I lay back down and slept.

But it was in those very minutes that the catastrophe occurred.

*

It was Bugge who woke me early the next morning. I'm usually an extremely deep sleeper once I get going, and he had to shake me pretty brutally to wake me up. I tried for as long as possible to brush him off by turning demonstratively to the other side and pulling the blanket over my head. But it was no good, he obviously wasn't going to give up. Finally I sat up and looked at him with an aggrieved expression.

'Just what do you think you're doing?' I exclaimed in a thick, grumpy voice. 'Don't you know I gave explicit instructions not to be woken up? What the hell . . . ?'

I stopped when I caught a glimpse of his face. I got a little shock and just sat there gaping in astonishment. He was totally changed. His charming, stony-faced mask was suddenly gone; his expression was one of real terror. Never before or since have I seen my friend so agitated.

'You have to get up right now,' he said in a voice that trembled slightly. 'Something terrible has happened.'

'What's the matter?' I felt a little tremor in my chest, an anxious foreboding.

'Gran has vanished.'

'Vanished? Gran?'

'Yes. During the night. And I'm afraid that something awful has happened to him. Or rather, I'm quite sure of it. Get dressed. We have to go and search for him as soon as possible.'

I felt dizzy as I pulled on my clothes. The memory of last night's little interlude came back to me. I recalled the footsteps I had heard, and that faint scream out in the woods. So it had been a real scream after all. Gran had gone out in the dark and had suddenly been taken by surprise by something terrible out there – *he* was the one who had screamed. I couldn't shake the feeling that it had finally happened, what I had been waiting a long time for – and feared. The expression on Bugge's face convinced me. The catastrophe had occurred, the lightning had struck.

We went into the living room, where the other three were gathered. It was obvious from looking at them that they already knew what had happened; they were clearly upset. Mørk in particular seemed to be terribly distressed and was pacing back and forth restlessly with his hands in his pockets. Liljan's complexion was ashen and the corners of her mouth were twitching. Even my wife had remarkably little color in her face. Bugge went straight to the front door and opened it.

'We have to get going right away,' he said drily.

We walked silently along the road towards the lake. Bugge led the way, walking a couple of steps ahead of the rest of us. Our course was set; there was no doubt about which direction to go, or in any case Bugge seemed to know where he was headed. When we had gone thirty or forty yards into the woods, he stopped at a little trail leading off to the left.

'We'll take this path,' he declared. 'It's a shortcut.'

We obeyed his orders and followed him. I found it a little strange that he should choose that particular path. I knew it led to a certain point on the shore, but how could he be sure that was where we should go? How could he be so certain it was a shortcut?

After a couple of minutes' march we arrived at the water. It lay dead and muddy before us in the gray morning mist; an unclean odor rose up from it, a damp smell of decay. There was an ominous silence around us. The birds were quiet; only a low, humming sound of insects vibrated in the air. A swarm of mosquitoes hung directly over the water like a noisy, unmoving veil, a tiny organ playing a single ugly chord. Some large spider-like creatures darted back and forth over the surface, cutting tears in the thick crust. I had never felt such an intense aversion to that place as I did now.

Bugge took several steps along the shore and looked searchingly into the water until he suddenly stopped short. Then he stood calmly, stretched out his arm, and pointed.

'There he is.'

He lay in a shallow part of the lake, just beyond a low ledge; we could hardly see him down in the blue-green darkness. His body was twisted as if in a violent spasm, and he was entwined on all sides in reeds – green, sticky grass that wound itself around his arms and legs. His face was turned upwards and his eyes were wide open. It looked as though he were staring at us.

None of us said anything. It was a dreadful moment, and as for me, my entire body felt numb, but all the same it didn't affect us as strongly as it might have under other circumstances. In a certain sense we had already known for several minutes that this was coming. The main shock was out of the way; it didn't come as a surprise out of nowhere. Bugge, standing at the edge of the ledge, had once again assumed his cold, impassive mask. Mørk was no longer so restless either. He had a relaxed expression, a fatalistic calm, as if he were only observing something inevitable. Sonja was still pale and stood next to me breathing heavily.

'Good God,' she whispered. 'Good God.' But there was no panic in her voice; it was composed, she had control over herself.

What astonished me most was the sight of Liljan. I had expected her to faint from the shock, but instead she seemed downright *relieved*. The color had come back to her cheeks, and life had returned to her dull eyes. She looked as though she had suddenly been freed of a great burden, she breathed more freely. How could she take it like that? Hadn't Gran been her friend, her most intimate friend?

Bugge broke the silence and took the initiative.

'We can't just stand here gawking,' he said. 'You two help me get him up. In the meantime, it might be best if the ladies stand back a little.'

Gran was lying about five feet below the surface. Bugge and I had to take off our clothes to dive after him, while Mørk assisted us up on the shore. It wasn't an easy task. The water was ice cold, and the bottom gave way under our feet like we were walking on quicksand. I thought that if Gran's body hadn't gotten so entangled in the tough reeds, he would have kept sinking down through the mud, and we never would have found him. After a great deal of effort, we finally managed to pull him up onto land. His lifeless body was almost completely stiff when we laid him down.

We got dressed again, and I stood silently for a while, looking at the dead man. His face had taken on a mechanical look; his expression could be seen much more clearly here in the light of day. It wasn't the relaxed, peaceful death mask so often seen on those who have drowned. His face was totally contorted, his mouth half open as if in a silent scream; his eyes expressed terror. And I felt that it wasn't just an ordinary fear of death in that face. It was fear of something else, fear of the unfathomable.

'This is what I warned you about yesterday,' Mørk suddenly put in, with a strange, hoarse voice. 'You should have listened to me instead of going on with this crazy game. There's a price to pay when the uninitiated try playing around with the great beyond. Hundreds of so-called spiritualists have met the same fate – men like Ludwig Dahl, for example.* I refer you to my article in *The Scourge*, number 4, 1937: "Spiritualism as a Parlor Game". It was an unpardonable stupidity not to leave this place last night.'

Bugge shrugged.

'You can save yourself the role of the Prophet Ezekiel,' he said drily. 'There was no way we could have gotten back to the city last night. You can't go on foot from here to Oslo in a storm like that one.'

'No, it's obviously better to wait until the lightning has struck,' Mørk said scornfully. 'You were probably thinking of staying here a bit longer yet, weren't you? Until none of us are left?'

'Of course.' Bugge was leaning over the body, examining it. 'If we had no reason for being here before, we do now at any rate. Something has happened here that obliges us to behave like grown-ups for once.'

'Then you insist on continuing our stay here?'

'Yes.'

Mørk took a step towards Bugge and looked at him accusingly.

'There's one sin that's worse than all the others, worse than adultery and murder, worse than treachery and dishonesty, even worse than writing modern fiction. And that is stupidity. *Stupidity* is the most unforgivable of all vices, the cardinal sin itself, an offense against the holy spirit. Kai Bugge, you are *stupid!*'

Bugge coolly continued his examination of Gran's body as if he hadn't heard Mørk's reply. I broke the awkward pause:

'Do you think he could have been – murdered? Do you see any signs of violence on his body?'

'No.'

'Then it looks like he threw himself into the water of his own free will?'

Bugge didn't answer. But I realized that his silence meant a confirmation. So Gran had become the second victim of Blue Lake's pull – or rather the third; Liljan had only been saved by pure chance. He too had been possessed, *he*, the most clear-headed of all of us. I suddenly understood why he had been behaving so strangely the past few days, why he had seemed so withdrawn and unapproachable. It wasn't only because of Bugge's flirtation with Liljan, although that might have played a role too. First and foremost he had acted that way because a strange and fantastic mood had crept up on him – he had felt the indescribable urge drawing him to the lake. That night he had gone there, driven by an inner impulse. He had stood and stared down in the moon-glittering water, he had felt the maelstrom down in the depths, that invisible sucking force. Then suddenly he couldn't restrain himself any longer; the possession had totally overwhelmed him. He had screamed in fear, wild, desperate fear. He had thrown himself into the vortex . . .

I was able to talk privately with Bugge a while later. He looked tired, his brow creased with worry.

'Mørk has a certain right to blame me,' he admitted. 'I should have known this was imminent. It was a terrible mistake not to have stayed with Gran last night; then this obviously wouldn't have happened. But now it's too late.'

'I think you can rest easy,' I said. 'It wouldn't have made any difference if you had spent the night somewhere else, you wouldn't have woken up in any case. I tried to wake you once last night, but it was no use: Sleeping Beauty's slumber was just a light afternoon nap compared with yours.'

'Really?' He seemed to cheer up. 'That makes me feel better. You get tired when you use your head a lot; thinking is the best sleeping aid. To tell the truth, I've been giving my cerebral cortex quite a workout the past few days.'

There was a question on the tip of my tongue.

'How could you be so sure that something had happened to Gran, just because he didn't happen to be in the house? He could have been out on a solo morning hike, couldn't he? And how did you know exactly where to find him? You found the way immediately, after all.'

My friend gave me a strange look.

'Liljan told me,' he said.

'I beg your pardon?' My eyes opened wide. 'Liljan? Then she must have gone to the lake earlier and found him?'

'No. Liljan hasn't left the house at all. The rest of us haven't either.'

'What are you saying? Then how could she have known that Gran – ? Maybe she has supernatural powers?'

Bugge nodded. There was an undertone of wonder in the sober voice:

'You might well call it supernatural. Liljan does in fact have some rather extraordinary abilities.'

CHAPTER TWELVE

In which we go for reinforcements

AFTER A SHORT DISCUSSION, we decided to visit Sheriff Bråten.

'There's really nothing for him to do here,' Bugge maintained. 'Policemen are no use in this sort of case. Their business should be limited to patrolling the streets and arresting vagrants. But perhaps it's our civic duty to warn him in a situation like this.'

We managed to carry Gran's body into the living room, and then all five of us set off down the road towards the village. Bugge and I walked a little ahead of the others, while Mørk, Sonja, and Liljan carried on a lively conversation a few yards behind us. I couldn't really hear what they were saying, but I could tell that Mørk was talking nonstop about his views on what had happened, and both Liljan and my wife were hanging on every word the entire time. Mørk is a misogynist, of course, and as a result he's very popular with the weaker sex; there's nothing women find more flattering than being despised.

I couldn't get my mind off what we had just gone through either.

'Is it possible Gran had a good reason for taking his own life?' I asked.

'If he had a reason, it could only be described as a bad one,' Bugge remarked drily. 'Besides, I believe our friend was a little too clear-headed to want to commit suicide.'

'But you don't think he was pulled in by the lake? Just like Werner? And Liljan, who had a narrow escape?'

'No.'

'What's the explanation, then?'

'It's very simple. Harald Gran was murdered. Someone pushed him into the water.'

I had almost expected him to say that; I didn't feel particularly surprised. But the very idea of it seemed inconceivable to me.

'How can you just assume something like that?'

'I've focused on one important detail. When I went through Gran's clothes just now, I found a small blackjack in his pocket; he normally didn't carry on him. If he had been possessed by the lake and had fallen victim to its peculiar attractive force, he would hardly have taken a weapon with him when he left. You remember Liljan's condition when she walked to the lake? Gran wasn't in the same state. A sleepwalker doesn't arm himself.'

'But why should Gran carry a weapon?'

'To be ready to defend himself against a purely physical opponent, a person of flesh and blood. After all, Harald has been convinced the whole time that he was hunting for a murderer, and he counted on meeting that person in the woods last night. He went out in the darkness consciously and deliberately to catch his prey. Unfortunately he underestimated the enemy.'

I shuddered.

'In that case, it was an awfully rash thing to do,' I muttered. 'He should have woken us up and asked us to go with him.'

'Certainly. But he's always had a bit of a Nick Carter complex. He wanted to crack the case single-handed, like the great detective.'

'I just don't understand how he could have been so sure he would find the murderer last night, of all nights.'

'Is your memory that bad? We'd just had a visit from that eccentric guest of ours, and the rainstorm provided the perfect opportunity to follow his footprints in the softened soil. Gran wanted to go in pursuit while the tracks were still fresh. What's more, I think a little light bulb went off for him yesterday, when he said he saw how it all fit together. He had unwittingly stumbled on the right solution, and he felt a burning desire to prove his theory at once. It's a shame it cost him his life.'

I walked on for a while, trying to collect my thoughts.

'But how did this alleged murder actually happen?' I said. 'After all, you claimed his body showed no signs of violence. A person doesn't drown in shallow water, just like that.'

'No, not just like that. But he could have been surprised from behind while he was standing for a moment by the shore; the other person could have crept up on him carefully and given him a violent shove. As you'll recall, he said himself the other day that he was a lousy swimmer, and even Johnny Weissmuller might flounder if thrown headfirst into cold water. He might have lost his breath, had his lungs fill with water, and gotten stuck in the mud and reeds. He probably drowned in the span of a few seconds. Actually, it's possible he died of shock. You remember the expression on his face, don't you?'

'Yes, I won't easily forget that.'

'It wouldn't be the first time someone died of fright.'

I noticed I was still pretty weak in the knees; my legs quivered slightly as I walked. It irritated me a little for Bugge to see how miserable I felt.

'Do you believe this creature, this murderer, wants to do away with more of us? You and me, for example?'

'It's not unlikely.'

'But who is he? Who is this man with the wooden leg, this monster of the woods, who is sneaking around up here for some reason and has already taken two lives? If you really know, is there any reason for being so damned secretive? Could it be the deranged murderer – the one who escaped from jail down in the village? I can't think of any other possible explanation.'

My friend brushed a fly from his cheek with a lazy movement of his hand.

'You're quite right in wanting to find out, Bernhard. Your curiosity is certainly justified. Just between you and me, I hope to be able to give you the answer tonight. If all goes right, I'll be able to show you the drama's final act.'

'And what happens in the final act?'

'You'll get to see the murderer up close – in a very interesting final scene.'

'Tonight?'

'Yes, the night of August 22, or more precisely, just after midnight on the 23rd. The same night Tore Gruvik killed himself exactly 110 years ago. A rather significant date, in other words. According to Bråten we can expect, among other things, to hear Gruvik's death scream coming from the lake.'

I cast a sidelong glance at him. He didn't seem to be pulling my leg.

'I can't quite figure you out,' I said. 'A moment ago you thought you'd found a natural explanation for everything that's happened, you claimed that a person of flesh and blood was behind it all. And now you start referring to that old story about Tore Gruvik again. What do you really think?'

Bugge gave an obliging smile.

'You'll understand that before the night is through.'

We arrived at the sheriff's house around 11:00 a.m. He gave us a warm welcome, shook hands with all of us, and invited us inside.

'Nice of you to visit me,' he said. 'It's not often people come to see a lonely old sheriff. By the way, how are you enjoying your stay at the haunted lake?'

'It pretty much lives up to its reputation, thanks,' I said. 'Although so far only one of us has died.'

'What do you mean? Where's Gran?'

'I'm afraid he's dead. Drowned in Blue Lake, just like the recipe calls for. That's the reason we've come to see you.'

'Good heavens! I don't believe it.'

He sank down into a chair and ran his hand across his forehead. The color drained from his face for a moment.

'How did it happen? And when?'

I told him what we knew – or what I myself had found out, anyway. I think I told the story pretty colorfully, and you could see it made a fairly strong impression on him. He and Gran had been students together, after all.

'It's quite peculiar,' he exclaimed when I had finished. 'It's really peculiar that this should happen just now. Did you know that I just arrested that insane fugitive?'

'When?'

'Yesterday morning. He simply walked down to the village and turned himself in. And can you guess why? He didn't dare stay in the woods any longer. According to his vague and somewhat rambling account, he had met a figure near Blue Lake the night before: a tall, gray, and supposedly transparent figure that was evidently dragging one of its feet. He was convinced it was Tore Gruvik he had seen. As far as I can gather, he didn't run across any of you. He was as terrified as a child, and under no circumstances did he want to remain on the loose a single day longer. He was pretty crazy before, but now he's gone completely off his rocker . . .'

Bråten lit his pipe and drew several thick, stimulating clouds of smoke into his lungs. I thought about it. If this guy had been arrested yesterday morning, then it couldn't have been him I had seen in the woods last night, nor could he have been the one in my room during the thunderstorm, a possibility I had counted on. Besides, he too had met the other one, the creature with the wooden leg, the monster of the woods . . . I wasn't the only one who had seen such things.

'I have to say, it's an odd coincidence,' Bråten continued, 'that Gran should have drowned in the lake shortly after that figure appeared nearby. You'd almost be tempted to believe there was something to that old legend. I don't put much stock in the words of madmen, but I have to admit that – '

'It goes without saying that the most reliable accounts of such phenomena come from insane people,' Mørk interjected. 'The mentally ill often have the ability to see into the other world; they have a spiritual eye that so-called normal people lack, simply because normal people don't *dare* to be anything but blind – '

'Very possible,' muttered Bråten. 'I don't know too much about that kind of thing.'

Bugge had sat in silence for a while, looking at his hands. Now he turned to the sheriff.

'Actually we came here to ask you for a little assistance,' he said. 'You have a car at your disposal, don't you?'

'Yes. I've got an old contraption that runs when you crank it up.'

'If the roads are passable, maybe you could help us drive our late friend down to the station tomorrow. We can't very well leave him lying around up here.'

'I'd be happy to.'

'Are you thinking of going back tomorrow?' I asked Bugge.

'There will be no need to stay any longer. One more thing, Bråten: I'd like to ask you to come back with us today. I'd appreciate it if you spent the night with us at the cabin.'

'With pleasure. Do you think I can be of some use?'

'Absolutely.'

'Maybe you have a definite theory about what happened?'

'Yes. And I also have a definite theory about what's going to happen. I'd suggest that you bring a gun with you.'

Bråten looked surprised.

'A gun?'

'Yes. You may end up needing it.'

'So you think it was *murder*? And that the murderer is still out there in the woods?'

'Bravo. You have an exceptional ability for putting two and two together, my dear Bråten.'

We stayed for a nice lunch with the sheriff, and the few hours we spent at his house were enjoyable, under the circumstances. It was late afternoon when we traveled back in his car. It wasn't exactly an ideal road for an old Chevrolet; the ascent was rather steep in places, and the chassis rattled ominously with every bump. We didn't make it all the way either, having to park the car on the side of the road a few hundred yards below the cabin.

When we came up to the little clearing, I stood for a few seconds looking at the house. In a way there was something almost alive about it as it stood there before us in the drowsy afternoon sun. The pale light formed weird reflections on the dark window glass, and the panes stared like enormous pupils towards a fixed point in the landscape. All was completely quiet. And yet a certain unease hung over the place, an inner tension, like there was something in the very walls . . .

The front door was open; we had apparently forgotten to close it. The moment I stepped over the threshold into the living room, something made me stop short: it was the same atmosphere Werner had described in his diary. I knew instinctively that someone must have been there while we were away. I carefully examined the various objects in the room. There was no doubt: something had changed since we left the place that morning. It seemed to me that the large table was in a different position, some of the chairs had been moved, and a book which had lain open on the fireplace mantel was now closed.

My discovery was confirmed by Sonja in an unexpected way. She had made a little trip into the kitchen and suddenly came running back with an astonished look on her face.

'I don't get it,' she cried. 'A bunch of food is gone. A box of canned goods has disappeared. And a loaf of bread. And a lot of butter . . .'

We stood staring at each other for several moments. Then Bugge gave a little whistle.

'Aha,' he exclaimed. 'Our anonymous guest has really begun to make himself at home. The ghost got hungry and thought it would be wise to stock up on supplies. I can't blame him – there's not much in the way of food on the astral plane. Incidentally, I didn't know ghosts had a taste for Bjelland's fish balls. But maybe our deceased friend intends to materialize sometime in the course of the evening.'

Mørk looked at him with contempt.

'You're talking like a schoolboy,' he said. 'Damn it, aren't you ever going to grow up?'

Personally, I didn't see how this episode was cause for amusement. I found it downright creepy that we'd had another visit from that fellow from the woods. He was obviously circling our cabin like a moth around a candle. But Bugge does have his own way of reacting to things.

The mood was tense that evening. I had the feeling the whole time that something was imminent. Something was being prepared, and I had an intuition that Bugge was the orchestrator. He had once again taken on that energetic, alert attitude that comes over him on certain rare occasions. He seemed to be pulling strings, moving unseen machinery; he reminded me of a chief of staff.

He didn't have much time for Bråten. Our guest kept trying to press him for more details about his murder theory, but Bugge always answered evasively. Finally the sheriff proposed that we patrol the area and track down the person who, as we now knew, must be somewhere in the woods, maybe even quite close to the cabin. Bugge rejected the proposal.

'We've already made a couple of attempts,' he declared. 'And it's completely hopeless. It's like looking for a needle in a haystack. Or trying to find a sensible remark in one of Mørk's articles.'

The job of entertaining Bråten fell to me. I realized he must be a little confused. He couldn't possibly have a clear idea of why Bugge would drag him up here like it was a matter of life or death, if his intention was only to ignore him. His voice had a slightly irritated tone when he spoke. Personally, I could easily understand his annoyance. At times Bugge's behavior can be totally outrageous.

My friend started to concentrate his attention on Liljan in an even more conspicuous way than before. He drew her aside with him into a remote corner of the room and talked with her for a long time, certainly over an hour. It was clearly not ordinary chitchat. They both seemed intensely preoccupied with each other; the conversation had to be about something extremely important. They talked so low that it was hard for me to catch much of what they said; only on one occasion was I able to pick up several sentences.

'I saw it all so clearly,' I heard Liljan say. 'Right after I dived into the water, I saw him coming after me. He leapt from the same ledge and followed me into the depths. This time I could make out his features clearly, I recognized him. And the whole time I had an odd feeling, like I was staring into the future, that this was something that would take place the following night.'

'In other words tonight?'

'Yes.'

'I understand. That fits perfectly.'

It was hard for me to concur with Bugge's last remark. What was it he understood? And what was it that fit so perfectly?

After concluding this rather unusual conversation, he went over to talk confidentially with my wife. He led her over to the same corner and was clearly trying to convince her of something. I secretly watched their facial expressions. It looked as if Sonja was strongly reluctant at first, but later let herself be talked into it. She yielded obediently to him; he obviously must have some kind of hypnotic power over her too. Under normal circumstances, I might have thought Bugge was making a pass at her – I sometimes have trouble trusting my friends – and I wouldn't have hesitated to intervene and break up their discussion. But it dawned on me that Bugge had other intentions. He was staging a drama, giving her an important role, *instructing* her. There was presumably no compelling reason for me to interfere.

A little later that evening, when I made a trip to the kitchen to grab a couple of bottles of beer, I found Sonja there preparing dinner. For the first time I observed signs of real anxiety in her. She was paler than usual, and I noticed her hand shook slightly as she handled the bread knife.

'What's the matter, darling?' I asked, surprised. 'Are you scared about something?'

'No, not at all.' She seemed evasive.

'You have stage fright, my dear. Do you think I can't see through my own wife? I haven't seen you this anxious since you took the stage as a half-naked extra in *Women* a few years ago.'

'I might have smoked too many cigarettes.'

'Honestly, little wife, spit it out. There's something brewing here tonight, isn't there? I saw you talking with Bugge.'

'No, it's nothing, Bernhard. You mustn't be so terribly curious. Anyway, it's not so strange if I don't feel quite myself after everything that's happened the past few days. With Werner. And Liljan. And Gran.'

'Goddamnit!' I exclaimed in annoyance. 'Why am I always kept in the dark whenever anything happens? I'm literally kept in quarantine. Am I really so untrustworthy?'

'Not at all, my dear. You're a very sweet and charming boy. Hand me those cups, would you?'

'Not a chance,' I said emphatically. 'A woman who keeps secrets from her husband doesn't deserve for him to hand her cups. So long.'

I took a beer under each arm and walked firmly back to the living room.

CHAPTER THIRTEEN

In which it is midnight, August 23

B Y II P.M., our little group was already gradually starting to break up. Sonja and Liljan were tired and went
to bed in Liljan's room, and Mørk also retired for the night.
For the past few hours he'd been in a visibly belligerent
mood and had behaved about as sociably as an Egyptian
mummy. Bråten, Bugge, and I remained sitting and chatting in front of the fireplace. Our guest gradually thawed
when Bugge once again started to show his friendlier side.
The two of them exchanged their views on their mutual
interest, criminology, and the sheriff told a couple of compelling stories from his experiences as a policeman. It was
really quite cozy sitting there in the warm glow from the
burning pine logs. I sat sucking on an old pipe I had found,
while I looked into the flames and tried to project myself
into a state of nirvana. There would have been an exqui-
sitely peaceful, vacation-like mood at that moment, if I
hadn't had that restless itching in my blood the whole time,
almost as if a little nail were constantly pricking my veins.
I couldn't shake the feeling that this peace was only the
calm before the storm. The atmosphere was still charged
with electricity; it hadn't yet broken out into a cleansing
thunderstorm.

Every so often I looked over at Bugge to see if I could
catch the slightest sign that he was worried too. Hadn't
he predicted that we would witness the drama's final act
tonight? If – as I thought – he was really the one setting the
scene, pulling the secret strings, shouldn't he be feeling an

almost unbearable tension? If so, he was managing to hide it well. He looked almost apathetic; his expression was as cold and imperturbable as an Indian brahman's, and nothing in his voice betrayed him. He spoke in the tone of an old, experienced radio host.

Outside night had fallen. A blue, caressing August darkness embraced the landscape, spreading out over the world like a soft, ethereal blanket. I got up from my chair and walked over to the open window. A gentle gust of the autumn night air blew into the room, a scent of the lushness of nature, of the dying summer. I've always felt an almost unhealthy lust for life on autumn evenings like that one, maybe because that smell is so reminiscent of death. It's the bittersweet odor of decay, the feverish aroma of corruption. But I had never known it as strong as it was then; I experienced it with all of my senses. Tonight fate was in the air, tonight something was going to perish. An almost inaudible tone quivered in the darkness, a rustling from up in space, like an invisible mill grinding among the stars. It was the night of August 22, one of the loveliest nights of the year . . .

Bugge glanced at his wristwatch.

'A quarter to midnight,' he said. 'It's almost the witching hour.'

He got up and sauntered over to me with his hands in his pockets. There was a little smile at the corner of his mouth.

'Well, Bernhard, how do you feel? Are you ready?'

'Ready for what?'

'To meet Tore Gruvik. I thought we'd go for a moonlight stroll and take a peek at him. You know I promised you that a rather compelling scene would be played out at the lake tonight. You won't be bored.'

'Do you mean we're going to the lake – now?'

'Yes. We'd better get a move on. We want to get there in

time. It would be a shame if we arrived too late – we won't see another performance like it in our lifetime.'

As I've said, I've never been a particularly brave man. I'm not the type to climb dizzying mountain peaks, or roll down Niagara Falls in a barrel, solely for the pleasure of dying young. I've never found danger a temptation; I've always preferred living like a mouse to dying like a lion. And I think I can safely say that there are things that have tempted me more than Bugge's proposal.

'To be honest, I don't really feel like . . .' I began cautiously.

'Come on, Bernhard, surely you're not scared of a respectable old ghost? I guarantee he won't do you any harm. In fact, he'll be rendered totally harmless before the night is through.'

'In that case there's no need for *me* . . .'

My friend got an almost malicious glint in his eyes.

'Are you coming?' he said. 'Yes or no. If you don't come, I'll have to go alone.'

There's one thing worse than fear itself, and that's the fear of appearing afraid. It's such a force in people's lives that it makes them do the stupidest things. It makes them cast aside all inhibitions, it makes them into *heroes*. You have to be an unusually big coward in order to become a real hero.

'Of course I'm coming,' I said.

Bråten had stood up too.

'Am *I* not allowed to take part in this expedition?' he asked. 'It sounds positively exciting.'

Bugge turned towards him. The little smile had vanished from his face; he looked as serious as an infantry captain the moment before an attack.

'I'd rather you stayed behind here at the cabin, Bråten. I have a little job for you.'

'What's that?'

'Simply to look after the house for the next half hour. There's a slight possibility a guest may come to visit while we're away; if so, you shouldn't forget your skills as a policeman. You mustn't allow that guest too much freedom. It's possible he wants to murder someone here.'

Bråten nodded. 'I understand.'

'Don't be scared to use your revolver. Even if it might seem a little impolite and lacking in hospitality.'

'Okay. Rest assured, you can count on me. He'll get a grand reception if he comes; I'll make sure he's taken care of properly.'

Bråten patted his jacket pocket with a smile and sat down again by the fire. It looked as though he relished the thought of a little one-on-one with a murderer. I felt reassured looking at him. He was massively built and had an obvious authority and self-confidence; it was clear he was no novice in his profession. I was glad we had brought him with us.

Bugge walked to the door.

'All right. Let's get going, Bernhard. See you later, Bråten. In this world or the next.'

We went out and Bugge shut the door carefully behind us. He grabbed my arm and held me back for a moment.

'It's possible we're being watched,' he whispered. 'It's best we play a little hide-and-seek. We need to try to make it into the woods as unobserved as possible. We'll make use of the terrain, as it's called in military speak, and sneak along the wall of the house. There's a path here, just to the right.'

'Do you know the way?'

'Of course. Come on.'

We crept carefully around the corner of the house and had to move in open country for a moment to reach the woods. I didn't feel so well during that moment, knowing my figure must stand out clearly in the bright moonlight.

I instinctively hunched over a little; what I really wanted was to lie flat on the ground and crawl. But a couple of seconds later we were safely in the thicket. Bugge walked a few yards ahead of me, moving with light, springy steps, the way you walk through a room where people are sleeping. I was annoyed with myself for not wearing sneakers. My soles clomped hard against the ground, and the stiff leather made a loud, unpleasant squeak every time I bent my foot. A couple of times, I stepped on branches lying across the path and it made an infernal racket; to my ears it sounded as loud as a large tree toppling over.

The moon hung white and heavy above our heads, partly hidden behind a thin lacework of clouds. It shone more intensely tonight than ever before, glowing with an ice-cold fire, like a frozen sun. The pale light slipped through the darkness of the woods lustfully, licking the barren ground along the tree trunks. The gray-white branches quivered slightly in the night wind, as if trembling from an inner chill. Once again nature was in a fever, once again there was something moaning here in the darkness, something clenched in spasms. The stars flickered nervously up in the heavens.

My dark shadow danced on the path in front of me. It looked like a strange, insubstantial being that followed me the whole time, step by step, parodying my movements, caricaturing my body's rhythm, mocking me with silent gestures. As I walked, staring at it, it suddenly occurred to me that it also had a *face*. A laughing, evil face with two narrow eyes and a mouth stiffened into a cold grin.

I quickened my pace to catch up with Bugge. I didn't want to walk alone anymore; I needed to feel another human being close beside me. Was it any wonder if people went crazy from living alone in a forest like this one?

He turned towards me for a moment. I may have been mistaken, but I thought he'd actually gone a shade paler than usual. I wasn't certain; it could also have been an effect of the moonlight.

'Well, Bernhard, are you enjoying yourself? Isn't it a fine night?'

'Thanks, it's not so bad. Although I can remember off the top of my head at least two nights when I've had more fun.'

'I wouldn't write tonight off until the sun comes up, if I were you. There's still a long way to go before the rooster crows. The lake's straight ahead of us now. We turn off to the left here.'

We left the path and started to make our way as carefully as possible through some dense bushes. It was a rather unpleasant hike; I had never been much for jungle adventures. The stiff twigs scratched my cheeks till they bled, and several times a branch hit me hard in the face. Maybe I was being ridiculously overimaginative in those minutes, but I had the constant feeling that it was nails *clawing* against my skin, and that it was a clenched human fist striking my cheekbones. I had to keep casting quick glances around me; the whole time I was expecting a strange being to dart out from the thicket, a tall, grayish figure without a clear shape, the same person I had seen by the lake.

I tried to stay as close on Bugge's heels as possible. The sight of his back was reassuring, and I noticed how smoothly his neck muscles worked each time he bent a branch aside. The past few days, I had discovered for the first time what it was that made Bugge superior. It was his almost uncanny mastery over his emotions, his unabashed self-confidence, his ability to make his way coolly and steadily towards his goal. What was the goal in this case? Did he know himself? Could he simulate a look of such certainty if he weren't holding all the threads in his hand?

'This is the place.'

We had stopped at the edge of the woods, several yards from the shore of the lake and a short distance below the little ledge from which Liljan had tried to jump when she was sleepwalking.

'We'll lie down here behind these bushes. This is an excellent vantage point; from here we have a view of all sides. Try to camouflage yourself as best you can.'

I obeyed Bugge's whispered orders and found a little hollow where I could lie down. There was a tickling in my teeth the whole time, a tingling, tense nervousness; I felt like an observer at the front lines. The enemy was within firing range, he might be just a stone's throw away. We lay motionless in the shadows, waiting for him to make a move. Beside me I heard Bugge's calm and even breathing.

The lake lay in cold, frozen tranquility before us in the moonlight. For the first time I noticed the odd way the water's surface reflected the light. It looked as though it came *from below,* as if the blue-white, shimmering reflection originated from a secret light source down in the depths, an underwater fire. But of course it was an optical illusion. The air was so clear that night and the moon shone brighter than usual; it was understandable that its rays could penetrate more deeply below the surface.

I don't know how long we lay silent beside each other in the darkness without anything happening. Maybe ten minutes, maybe fifteen. Gradually the night cold began to make itself felt; I started to shiver a little and had to rub myself every so often to keep warm.

'How many hours do you think we'll have to lie here waiting?' I whispered to Bugge. 'I've heard pneumonia is pretty unpleasant.'

'You mustn't be impatient, old friend. It won't be long now.'

I was startled by a noise right in front of me. But it was only a frog crawling to the shore. It was making slow, grotesquely human movements, dragging itself like a tiny hunchbacked gnome towards the water's edge, rustling through the moist grass. Suddenly it leapt into the air and disappeared into the lake with a disgusting little gurgle.

Quite a few more minutes passed, and I was starting to find this inaction more and more physically painful. The landscape around us was dead and unchanging; apart from the frogs' monotonous croaking there was no sign of life in the vicinity. I got a slight suspicion that this must be one of Bugge's usual eccentric whims. How could he be so certain that something was going to happen at the lake at this precise moment? Was there really any reason to stay at our uncomfortable post any longer?

'It appears your open air theater is going to be a flop,' I muttered. 'It doesn't look like the actors want to take the stage.'

'Just wait.'

'To be honest, I don't intend to wait much longer. I value my physical health.'

He was silent. I was starting to feel rather impatient.

'Did you hear what I said?'

But he didn't hear. He had suddenly raised himself up on his elbows and was looking in the opposite direction. All his senses were suddenly alert, as if at a signal, and he was staring intently towards the road leading to the cabin.

I rose up too, to find out what had caught his attention. In the next second I discovered what it was. And I had just enough self-control to stifle a frightened cry; only a weak groan escaped from my mouth.

A figure dressed in white was walking along the road. It slowly came closer, its arms stretched straight out in front as though groping for some invisible object. The steps were mechanical, like those of a sleepwalker . . .

It was a woman. It was Liljan, sleepwalking towards the lake for the second time!

A couple of seconds passed before I could collect my thoughts after the shock. Then I rose halfway up; I was getting ready to rush forward and stop her. But Bugge wheeled around, grabbed my shoulder hard, and pushed me down again.

'Lie still!'

I stared at him with an expression of the utmost confusion. Then I knocked his hand aside and again made a move to get up.

'Have you gone completely insane?' I exclaimed. 'Do you want ...'

'Lie still, you idiot!'

He hissed it in my face. And at the same time he caught my eye and looked at me with a gaze that radiated an almost fanatical willpower; flames shot from his pupils. It had a stunning effect on me, as if he'd given me a blow to the temple. I sank back and lay there passively, unable to move a muscle.

But at that moment the monstrous suspicion struck me again: Bugge was behind it all, *he* was the one practicing black magic here in the woods! *He* had bewitched Werner, *he* had murdered Gran, and at this very moment *he* was driving Liljan to her death. And here I was, an eyewitness to the tragedy – unable to intervene, lying powerless beside a monster!

I only took in what happened during the next few seconds as an unreal stream of impressions. My consciousness was dulled, I was in a state of pure apathy. Liljan came closer and closer to the edge of the lake, step by step. She was walking towards the little ledge. The moonlight cast a frozen glow on her white nightgown. She still had a few yards left to go ...

She stopped at the shore, right at the edge of the ledge. She stood there hesitantly for a few moments, as if suddenly warned by a voice within her. But then it was like an unseen hand pushed her in the back. She stumbled, lost her balance, and plunged forward into the lake. The water sprayed up around her; it looked like an enormous wet fist closing around her body and dragging her down. A cluster of bubbles rose up and burst on the surface.

I think I tried to yell, but I wasn't capable of making a single sound. My mouth was as dry as the desert sand, my tongue was paralyzed. The whole thing had to be a bad dream, a horrible nightmare. My lower jaw hung slack and my eyes were stiff and blind like two dead marbles in my head. I must have looked completely unhinged.

A minute passed. An endlessly long and dreadful minute, during which we just lay there beside each other in a hushed silence, almost without breathing. At least I couldn't hear Bugge breathing anymore, and I didn't dare turn around to look at him. I only knew he was lying there, a couple of feet away from me.

Then something happened that brought me back to my senses and made me immediately discard my suspicion of Bugge. That suspicion had been ridiculous, the result of a momentary confusion. A dry twig cracked nearby, a foot stepped on a branch. Something that must have been standing still in the darkness the whole time went into motion, began to maneuver carefully through the thicket. And immediately afterwards a human form emerged from the woods.

It was a man. He turned his back to us and walked slowly along the shore towards the little ledge. The instant I saw him, I recognized him. I knew him from his limping gait – it was the man I had seen at the lake the night before!

Bugge nudged me in the side.

'Final scene,' he whispered. 'Enter Tore Gruvik, stage left . . .'

The man had arrived at the ledge and stopped at the very edge of it. He stood there staring down into the water as if fascinated by his own reflection. This time I could make him out more clearly than before. There was something physical about that figure after all, something tangible; he no longer looked like a misty phantom. I got a good look at his defective foot for the first time. He didn't have a wooden leg at all, it was more like a clubfoot. I felt an icy chill run through me. Was this a living person or an apparition?

For half a minute he stood there in the semi-darkness as motionless as a statue. And then it happened. His body suddenly started to tremble, his limbs quivered, and he twisted as if having an epileptic fit. He lifted his face so that his features were clearly defined for a moment in the moonlight, and a sound broke from his throat, a harsh, piercing sound. There was white foam at the corners of his mouth; he *screamed*. Then it was like his legs suddenly couldn't hold him any longer. He collapsed to his knees, swung halfway around, and plunged sideways into the lake. A wave rose up foaming from the depths; the swell traveled in all directions, and a cold gust of wind blew across the landscape. The rings rolled out for a moment over the water's surface, becoming weaker and weaker until everything was dead and still like before.

We remained lying there for a while without doing anything. Finally Bugge stood up and brushed the pine needles off his clothes.

'Exit Tore Gruvik,' he said drily. 'The curtain falls.'

I was in no condition to stand up immediately. A loud buzzing filled my ears; I was completely exhausted from trembling, and at the same time I felt more surprised than ever before in my life. I had seen something that really forced me to doubt my own senses, something that pushed everything else I had experienced into the background. I had seen the revenant's face. When he had turned towards the moon for a moment, I had been able to make out his features for the first time. And I had recognized him.

It was Bjørn Werner.

Bugge reached out a hand to me.

'You have to get up, Bernhard. The performance is over now. Our mission is done, there's nothing more we can do here.'

I gave him an appraising look. He stood over me, as detached and phlegmatic as usual. His eyes had no trace of the strange expression from a moment earlier.

'Liljan!' I exclaimed. My voice sounded cracked and unrecognizable. 'What happened to Liljan?'

'Nothing. Absolutely nothing, I assure you. Liljan is sleeping soundly back at the cabin.'

'What do you mean? Surely I haven't started seeing pink elephants? I'm not hallucinating –'

'Of course not. You're about to understand how everything fits together. Some of it's fairly complicated, but nothing that a man of your mental abilities shouldn't be able to handle.'

I got to my feet. I was stiff and cramped like an old man; I felt as though I'd grown many years older in the span of a few minutes. We set off on our way back, this time taking the direct route. I kept having to lean on Bugge so I didn't topple over; one of my legs was still asleep, and the dizzy feeling hadn't gone away.

'You'll have to excuse me. I feel sort of like one of the survivors of the San Francisco earthquake,' I said. 'But that's pretty understandable, don't you think?'

My friend nodded.

'Do you feel groggy?'

'Groggy is putting it mildly. My head is like a field hospital after an air raid. How in the world does all this fit together? Was it really Werner the whole time –?'

'Yes. It was Werner who played the role of Tore Gruvik. It was Werner who killed Gran and tried to take his sister's life – using a method that's totally unprecedented in modern criminal history, by the way. And, finally, it was Werner who drowned himself tonight – and not until tonight.'

I shook my head.

'That doesn't make any sense. He's been dead and drowned a whole week. Bråten found his footprints . . .'

'. . . which stopped right at the edge of the lake and proved that he must have jumped in. But a good swimmer can climb back onto land somewhere else along the shore, right? Let's say fifty or sixty yards further down.'

'But the wooden leg?'

'That he'd fitted himself with? It was a fairly simple affair to mount a small wooden block under one of his boots, so that the tracks would seem to be Tore Gruvik's. Do you remember that sawed-off branch Gran found in the little shanty? And the saw with fresh scratches in the rust? It appears that's where he had his workshop.'

'Where could he have been hiding the whole time?'

'Here, there, and everywhere. He was probably always on the move. Now and then he might have taken refuge in one of the loggers' huts; other times he might have slept in one of the caves by the river. There are plenty of hiding places in the woods.'

I had to shake my head once more.

'This all sounds so wild,' I objected. 'Wildly improbable. What was his goal in doing all of this? A man who fakes his suicide with elaborate footprints and swimming exercises and then attaches a wooden leg to himself, a man who lives in caves by night and limps around like a ghost in the woods, a man who kills his friends and relatives without any trace of a motive – a man like that must be . . .'

'Quite right,' remarked Bugge. 'He must be mad.'

When we got back to the cabin, Sonja met us at the door. Her hair was wet and her teeth were chattering; she had wrapped herself up carefully in my robe and was rubbing herself as hard as she could, trying to get some warmth back in her body.

'It's really quite cold, going for a swim at this time of night,' she said.

'What?' I exclaimed. 'You don't mean it was *you* who . . . ?'

I suddenly realized that it was easy to confuse the two in the dark. Sonja and Liljan are remarkably similar in appearance, and now my wife had let her hair down over her shoulders like Liljan usually wears it. Furthermore, she had moved in exactly the same way when walking down the road: the outstretched hands, the sleepwalker-like steps . . .

'Your wife is an exceptional underwater swimmer,' Bugge declared. 'She gave us all a demonstration of it a couple of days ago. What's more, she's a talented actress, very good at taking direction. But above all, she's a really brave girl, as I pointed out to you on an earlier occasion.'

I went straight to the nearest chair and sat down. I fell into it with all of my weight – what was left of my 163 pounds.

'Please give me a drink,' I groaned. 'I would really like a drink before the ambulance comes for me . . .'

CHAPTER FOURTEEN

In which the veil is lifted

WE WERE ALL GATHERED in the living room in front of the fire once more – everyone but Liljan; she was still asleep, and Sonja insisted we shouldn't wake her. Bugge had just brought Bråten and Mørk up to speed on the latest events, and the sheriff in particular looked as if he couldn't believe his own ears. Which I for one could certainly understand.

'Now perhaps you'll be so kind as to lift the veil for us a little,' I said to Bugge. 'Surely you've played the role of sphinx long enough.'

'Gladly. I'll be happy to tell you everything I know.' He leaned back comfortably in his chair and folded his hands behind his head. 'I'm just not really sure where to begin . . .'

'There must be a beginning?'

'Of course. Let me begin at the beginning. Let me preface it with what's supposed to have happened here in these woods 110 years ago, the background for all of this, the Gruvik drama.

'I'm sure you all remember the facts of the story, but to be safe I'll summarize it so that we don't miss any details. Tore Gruvik was known as an eccentric in the village. He was considered an unusually evil man; he couldn't stand anyone except his sister, whom on the other hand he loved passionately. He kept her imprisoned, so to speak, at home on the farm and wouldn't put up with any men courting her. When that Don Juan arrived at the farm and ran off into the woods with his sister, he got furious, followed them up to the cabin, killed them both, and flung their bodies into the lake. A few days later he lost his mind and went the same way as his victims, drowning himself.

'According to the legend, Tore Gruvik returned after his death, possessing all those who tried to live in this house, filling them with his own madness and pulling them down with him into the lake. The local people claim this has happened several times over the years. It's a claim we can't really verify; it's probably a myth. But in any case we know that it applies in Werner's case – he suffered exactly the same fate described in the legend. In symbolic terms, you could in fact say that Tore Gruvik crept inside of him and drew him into the lake.'

Bugge paused and dug in his pocket for his cigarettes.

'But that's no explanation,' I exclaimed, disappointed. 'We've heard this before. It's almost the same as what Mørk always – '

'Of course it's no explanation. It's just a description, a superficial summary of what happened. Our real interest, however – or at least *mine* – is in identifying the mental mechanisms that made such a phenomenon possible – or rather, such a series of phenomena. And here I have to jump ahead a little.'

He had found his cigarettes, took his time lighting one, and enjoyed the first deep puffs.

'All of you – except for Bråten – have gotten enough psychological clues to enable you to form a working theory of the Werner case. You in particular, Bernhard, have been privileged in that regard. But this evidence probably passed right by you; it essentially consists of small, unremarkable details, trifles you would overlook unless you have a sharp eye for such things. I'd like to take one of those trifles as my starting point, namely one of Liljan's little stories about her brother.

'You might remember what Liljan told us on the train

ride up here – that her brother was once blindsided by a raging case of pneumonia and lay helpless on the floor of his apartment, unable to summon assistance. Suddenly she felt there must be something wrong with him, she knew he was in danger. She went to him at once, had to break into that tiny apartment of his, and managed to save him just in time.

'Now at this point we have to stop and add a question mark. How can we account for a person suddenly being able to "feel" in this way? Maybe we could chalk it up to the proverbial "woman's intuition"? Certainly, but that's no explanation whatsoever. We have to ask: what does it mean that Liljan, Liljan Werner of all people, had that kind of intuitive experience? And there we get an interesting answer, an answer that immediately brings us closer to the heart of the problem: *It means there was a strong telepathic connection between Werner and his sister.*'

Bugge leaned forward in his chair for a moment and raised his voice for the final sentence. He observed his listeners closely for a few seconds as if to see what effect his words had had. Then he settled back in his chair again.

'I'm sure there's no need for me to play teacher and prove to you that telepathy, long-distance mental communication between people, is in fact a reality. Hopefully you're all enlightened enough to accept that; anyway, there's a great deal of evidence to prove its existence. Among other things, I could refer to Harriet Bosse's edition of Strindberg's letters; a telepathic connection existed between the two of them for many years, and it continued long after their divorce. They knew everything about each other during that time, what the other was doing, even the most secret impulses and ideas were registered; the distance between them was irrelevant. But enough of these digressions, let's go on.

'So, then: Liljan knows that her brother is sick because

she has received his telepathic signal, his distress call in the darkness. But that brings a new problem to the forefront: in what situations is this sort of contact between two people possible? When can it arise? And the answer is close at hand, it's on the tip of our tongue: it arises when the two people are very closely in tune with each other – in other words, when they love each other.

'And now we come to the heart of the matter: Bjørn Werner loved his sister passionately, and she reciprocated his affection. This feeling was dominant particularly in *him*; it filled his life completely and has been the real driving force behind all his actions.

'Werner desired Liljan. But, regrettably, when a man falls in love with his own sister, he is prevented, for various reasons, from satisfying his inclinations. The causes aren't so much social and biological as they are of an internal, psychic nature; incest-fear stands in the way, a fear deeply rooted in the so-called Oedipus complex. It's all very tricky. Ibsen dealt with it in *Ghosts*, and we feel a slight chill of discomfort when the subject is broached; we'd rather not discuss it in polite company. Enough about that. Werner was prevented from having Liljan, she was taboo for him. But it wasn't something he could just switch off. She was the woman of his life, and that kind of love is *fate*; it's not something you can just drain out with the bathwater.

'A person who can't tear himself away from such fixations becomes what we call a neurotic. He lives in a small, closed world, the world of his own sickness. He replaces reality with fantasy; he runs after a make-believe goal and always winds up back at the starting point. He's doomed to circle in a fixed orbit around his innermost problem. It gradually becomes the center of his universe, everything else moves in relation to it. It's the condition people referred to in the old days as *bewitched*.

'How does a neurotic think?

'What a person loves but cannot have becomes a holy object, something that no one is allowed to touch. If no one else gets to enjoy it, then he keeps it all to himself – in a negative sense. And so Werner's relationship towards Liljan was determined: he decided that she must remain untouched; she would be taboo for other men too. In his mind she became the *pure* woman, the virgin. And on his side, he remained completely faithful to her, living an ascetic life like a Buddhist monk. His whole worldview was colored by it – for a while he even studied theology! His pronounced inclination to live as an idler was also an expression of that same ascetic lifestyle – he didn't want to betray her with anyone else, not even with that most dangerous rival of passion: work!

'But then he takes on an unusual interest: he becomes interested in philology, he gets caught up in Dante – that is, he starts to concern himself with the figure of Beatrice. One more little detail that fits into the overall psychological picture. He becomes obsessed with Beatrice because she is the embodiment of the sexually pure woman; she becomes his idealized image of Liljan. The way Dante describes his heavenly beloved is how Werner wants his sister to be. Notice how Werner puts it in his diary: he asserts that Dante's book is the only one a person can always come back to. It leads to redemption and *purity*; in other words, it leads to Beatrice. And he reproduces a couple of verses from the book, describing the poet's first meeting with his chosen one, who comes to him from regions of bliss. I'm hardly a great reader of poetry, but I think I'll try to recite the first lines anyway.'

Bugge reached over to the shelf above the fireplace and took down Werner's diary, which had been lying there the whole time. He paged through it until he found what he was looking for.

'Here it is:

'But before me stood *Beatrice*, the pure one,
    turned towards the beast which in itself unites
    with two natures one person alone.'

Bugge was certainly bad at reading aloud; an old, professional stage actor couldn't have done it worse. He snapped
the book shut and turned towards us again.

'What can these verses have meant to Werner? Why did
he focus on *these* lines in particular? Hardly out of enthu-
siasm for the verses' formal qualities – it's an unusually
clunky and awkward poem; hopefully it's the translator's
fault. No, he fixated on these lines because they're an exact
depiction of his own relationship with his sister. That was
how they stood in relation to each other in his neurotic
fantasy: on the one side, *her*, a symbol of chastity, perfec-
tion, sanctity; on the other side, *him*, "the animal" with
two natures in the same person – the platonic lover and
the murderer! That's how he unconsciously interpreted
it: he has a hidden nature, a criminal, inside him, and he
experiences this double nature when he stands face to face
with his Beatrice. She not only appeals to the noblest part
of him, she also awakens his criminal side!

'The catastrophe occurs. Gran shows up in the arena
and falls in love with Liljan; the two of them move into
an apartment together and start a relationship. Werner discovers this and is stunned. After all, it's the worst thing that
could happen to him. His Beatrice has suddenly toppled
down from the heavens, his Madonna has become a harlot!
He makes a desperate attempt to split them up, sending
vile, anonymous letters to both of them.'

'Was it really *him* who wrote the letters after all?' I
exclaimed. 'There, you see, Sonja! Remember what I said?
I'm pretty clever when it comes to –'

'Of course he wrote them,' Bugge went on. 'Who
else? But the attempt failed. And from that moment on,

the criminal urge gets stronger and stronger in Werner's subconscious. He would rather see Liljan dead than in the arms of another man, and he wants to kill the man who has been her lover. But that impulse is still repressed in him; he can't commit such an act while he's in his right mind. First he has to wipe out his consciousness, be flung out into madness. It's at just this moment that he travels to the cabin. *He is seeking out the situation that will drive him mad.* Of course it was no coincidence that he bought this house, of all houses, when he decided to buy a hunting cabin. He suspects what will happen to him here, and he *wants* it to happen; he can no longer resist the hidden forces that are driving him on.

'During his stay at Dead Man's Cabin he becomes possessed by the power of Blue Lake – just as described in the legend. *He is possessed because the Gruvik legend involves the basic motive in his own life.* In these dark, sinister regions his own subconscious fantasy once played out as reality: Tore Gruvik loved his sister and killed her because she betrayed him, and at the same time he killed the man who had dared to violate her sanctity. It's a perfect parallel. Gran had committed a sacrilege against Werner in exactly the same way: he had seduced Liljan, "gone off into the woods" with her. Werner associates the old drama with the surroundings where it took place; the ghastly atmosphere of the dark woods, the lake, the walls of the house, presses in on him – and fuses with his own neurotic fantasy: the murder of Liljan and Gran. His diary makes for compelling reading when it tells how he's slowly captured by the lake, that is, by the urge to repeat Tore Gruvik's actions, which had been committed right here at Blue Lake. He feels the whole time as though evil, external powers are toying with him, but in reality he's a victim of forces inside his own mind. The ghost he thinks he sees is only a symbolic hallucination; it's the symbol of his own criminal subconscious, the other nature in himself.

'This is shown clearly by one of the descriptions in the diary, the one where he's sitting by the lake, staring down into the water, and his reflection suddenly starts to alter. All of a sudden he discovers that it's an entirely different being he sees there: a bearded face with a low forehead and evil, brutish features, a person missing a foot, the leg ending in a short stump, a wooden leg. As might be expected, he's terrified. But this hallucination is fairly easy to analyze: the fact that the reflection changes just means that it's the changes of his own mind he's witnessing. He has seen himself turn into Tore Gruvik!

'He's in the process of identifying himself with that person, that murderer and suicide. Of course it happens after great mental struggles; his consciousness defends its last strongholds, but little by little it has to surrender. It's interesting to look at what sort of literature he was occupied with during the first days of his stay. First and foremost, Dante's *Divina Commedia*; his Beatrice complex is the driving force the whole time. Next Flaubert's *The Temptation of St Anthony*; he feels himself to be a sort of Anthony, a desperate hermit in the desert, an ascetic struggling against monstrous temptations. Finally Strindberg's *Inferno*; he too is at war with "powers", but the result of that struggle is different than in Strindberg's case: Werner is defeated – he winds up in total madness. On August 16 he leaves the cabin and sets out into the woods. From that moment on he goes entirely in the form of Tore Gruvik. In the deepest psychological sense he becomes a *revenant*.

'If you ask a patient at a mental asylum what his name is, you might, for example, get the answer "Alexander the Great". You shouldn't take it as some kind of bad joke; the person in question firmly believes that he is Alexander the Great, and his behavior is totally in keeping with that conviction. He could give detailed depictions of his experiences at the battle of Issus or tell you enthusiastically about the latest military triumphs he has celebrated with his cavalry and his Macedonian phalanx; he'll sit down and work out meticulous battle plans with an eye towards the conquest of India. In the same way Werner believes that he *is* Tore Gruvik; it's only logical for him to mount a sort of wooden leg under one of his feet. After all, the *footprints* played a central role in the old legend – no one ever saw the ghost itself, only its footprints.

'With a little cleverness, you could have – from the evidence just referred to – guessed it was Werner playing the role of the ghost. In the Gruvik legend, as Bråten told it, the old murderer was missing his *left* foot. But in the tracks we found in the woods and in Bernhard and Sonja's room, the prints from the wooden leg were on the *right* side. In other words, Werner remembered the story wrong, and that same mistake is repeated in the diary when he describes the reflection scene at the lake. There's only one conclusion to be drawn from that, right? I'm surprised that you, Bernhard, born and raised with crime novels on your bedside table, could really have missed such a subtle detail . . .'

I had been swept away by Bugge's account of the events. Little by little, I seemed to be seeing things in a new and clearer way. I was starting to glimpse the logical thread running through the chaos.

'Speaking of the diary,' I interjected, 'how could Gran insist that the handwriting on the final pages was different?'

'Because it *was* a different handwriting. I have nothing against graphology; it's of course reasonable to assume that a person's inner self is reflected in the way he writes. But handwriting isn't something fixed and unalterable. It's a sensitive instrument, it reacts like a seismograph does to subterranean tremors. And it's logical that it would react fairly powerfully during a crisis like this one.

'But now we come to the next chapter, the strangest and most original in the whole story. Namely the chapter in which Liljan barely escaped becoming a victim of the lake's "pull".

'Let me insert a parenthesis here. Liljan has been my patient for over six months; she has been going through analysis with me since early this year. Liljan suffered from a neurotic illness like Werner's; she had an unconscious erotic fixation on her brother. My task as analyst was to make that attitude *conscious* in her and thereby free her of it. Out of that analysis came – among other things – the two dreams that you learned about a few days ago, Bernhard. They play an important role in this connection – I'll come back to them in a moment.

'So, then: Werner is wandering around in the woods, insane. But for the time being he doesn't toss himself in the lake. He has "become" Tore Gruvik and must repeat his acts: he must kill his sister and his sister's lover before taking his own life. But how is he to summon them here? By arranging a suicide. He delivers a note to the sheriff, asking him to come and see him the following morning because he has important information to provide about the escaped criminal. When Bråten arrives, Werner has vanished, but his footprints lead to the shore of the lake, and his rifle and the body of his dog are also lying there. In short, everything points to his having done away with himself. But in reality he's only taken a fifty-yard swim and gone into hiding in the woods. He shot the dog because he obviously couldn't keep it with him – a dog isn't a particularly quiet animal – and on the other hand he couldn't send it away; sooner or later it would come sniffing around his hiding place and he'd be discovered. Besides, killing his dog made his suicide seem more probable, or Bråten drew that conclusion, at any rate.

'Werner suspected we would come and carry out this

expedition of ours. He knew that the "criminologist" Gran in particular would be interested in a riddle like this suicide. It may sound strange that a mentally ill person could have done something so methodically. But I've always spoken out against the idea that mentally ill people's behavior is senseless. On the contrary, psychopaths act *more* methodically than normal people; they obey the compulsive inner logic of their illness.

'Incidentally, this "suicide", this peculiar swim in the lake, also has a deeper psychological meaning. In Werner's fantasy, the lake symbolizes what is *criminal*: Tore Gruvik's actions, as well as the criminal side of his own subconscious. When he throws himself in the lake, it means, in other words, plunging into the unconscious, taking the plunge into crime. It's really also a kind of suicide; by doing it, he kills the conscious part of himself for good. From then on, he is a dead man, a revenant – from then on, he is Tore Gruvik!

'The most important thing for him in this situation is to summon his sister. And here he makes use of a means that proved infallible once before: he takes advantage of the long-distance mental connection that exists between the two of them – he summons her *telepathically*.

'Here the diary again provides a curious piece of evidence. We find a summary of two dreams, dated the 9th and 10th of August. Werner dreams that he sees a shining white lily in Blue Lake. It slowly floats under the shadow of a spruce tree, and at the very moment the shadow falls on it, the lily begins to wilt. He feels a violent urge to leap from the shore, grab hold of the flower and sink to the bottom with it. He does so, then feels the water close over his head; everything goes dark around him –

'In the next dream he's standing on the steps of a train and sees a young woman running towards him. He doesn't recognize her, but he knows her name is Beatrice. She's evidently being pursued, she shows every sign of terror. Werner focuses his whole willpower on her reaching the train before her pursuer catches up to her. He reaches his hand out towards her and pulls her into the carriage at the last moment. A second later, the train sets off.

'*Liljan and her brother had these dreams at the same time.* Or more accurately: the same dreams observed from different points of view. Liljan dreams she is drifting in a lake, naked, her body shining white and pure in the moonlight. She floats into the shadow of a spruce tree and immediately notices her body beginning to wither. Her hands and feet turn black and charred; it gradually spreads over her whole body, and she feels as though she has become leprous. Then she catches sight of a large, shaggy beast standing motionless on the shore and staring at her. She feels a strong fear, but at the same time a peculiar attraction towards that creature standing there looking into her eyes. She's totally hypnotized and can't move. Suddenly the beast leaps straight down onto her, grabs her tight, and pulls her down into the depths.

'Next she dreams that she is the woman being pursued. She's running towards a train, and there's a man standing on the steps who helps her up. She doesn't know who he is; his facial features are indistinct, but nevertheless she feels she knows him. She collapses to the floor exhausted when the train starts to go. She perceives that her pursuer is grasping at her clothes, but he doesn't get hold of her – she is saved. Oddly enough it's only *now* that the fear really sets in, and she awakens with a scream . . .

'*These dreams are telepathic signals from Werner to his sister.* At this point, while he's still at the cabin, he has already started summoning her. His psychopathic plan is to draw her down with him into the lake, into death. That's what the dreams are about.

'The dreams' meaning is simple: Liljan in Werner's

dream is a threefold symbol. First, she symbolizes purity, chastity – that's emphasized by the fact that the flower is so shining and white; second, she's a symbol of female sexuality; and third, the very word *lily* is derived from the name *Liljan*. In Liljan's corresponding dream, she herself is the lily; it's her own body that is white and pure, that is, sexually pure, before she drifts into the shadow of the spruce tree. Like the lily, this spruce, or *gran*, alludes to a name: Gran. It's Harald Gran who has "overshadowed" her and made her to "wither", made her "leprous", in other words, made her feel impure. Werner has to throw himself down on the lily and drag it to the bottom; that is, he must save his sister from her ignominy by killing her.

'The corresponding element in Liljan's dream is that a large, shaggy beast jumps down on her and pulls her underwater with it. In her psychoanalysis session, she has a single insight into this dream: she associates "a large, shaggy beast" with "a bear". This bear, or *bjørn*, is a play on her brother's name, Bjørn Werner. Further insight is denied to her; these dreams represent the turning point in the analysis, when resistance sets in. The analysis is touching on a forbidden area of her psyche – her attraction towards her brother.

'The second dream deals with the same theme. The running woman is Liljan. She's being pursued by a man who wants to desecrate her, and she's running in order to preserve her innocence. That it's Werner standing on the steps to help her up in the nick of time represents him saving her through death. The train journey is a death symbol, something we recognize from poetic usage: when a person dies, it's said that he has "set off on a long journey". That Liljan's fear doesn't really set in until *after* she is rescued on the steps is actually quite logical – it's the *fear of death* she's really feeling!

'Their inability to recognize each other in the dreams is

typical. Each of them is the cause of the other's neurosis, but such a cause is always *repressed*, and thus they can only see each other behind symbolic masks. It's especially typical that the woman in Werner's dream is called Beatrice; that shouldn't require any further explanation after what I said earlier.

'Let's get on with the story. It goes like Werner planned: we organize an expedition and set off for the cabin to shed light on what happened. Maybe he hadn't foreseen that there would be so many of us; no doubt he had hoped that only Liljan and Gran would come. The striking thing was that everything was set in motion by Liljan's initiative; after all, *she* was the one who had received her brother's signal! She *had* to come, just as she was driven by an inner need the time Werner was deathly ill with pneumonia.

'The first time we inspect the lake, something odd happens. Liljan stands there as though spellbound, staring at her surroundings. When she's asked what's wrong, she responds that she has a strange feeling of having been there before. It's clear this discovery makes an uncanny impression on her; it's like a faint memory is suddenly awakened to life, and she connects that memory with something dreadful.

'How can we explain such a phenomenon? Had she really seen that lake before?

'In a certain sense she had. *She recognized the landscape from the telepathic dream.* It was the exact visual impression Werner had – if you will – broadcast to her; the first dream took place at the lake, after all. That sheds new light on the mental contact between the two of them. It's not only the content of the simultaneous dreams that's the same, they also take place in exactly the same surroundings! Werner and Liljan, in other words, lived a sort of shared dream-reality, where they quite literally *met each other*. The case is definitely interesting; I've never come across an analogous example in the psychological literature. But my explanation is unquestionably the only possible one. And someone had to be the first to make such a discovery.

'After that episode we all suspected something was brewing with Liljan, that something was going to happen to her. And quite right – we got the sleepwalking scene. Unfortunately, at that point in time the *extent* of the danger wasn't clear to me; horror was only a hair's breadth away. Fortunately Bernhard was able to intervene and avert the catastrophe in the nick of time, an action for which he definitely deserves a little silver medal.

'According to Gran, Liljan had been a sleepwalker the entire time he'd known her. We pose the question automatically: why does a person walk in their sleep? Does it mean anything at all? If we operate from our scientific postulate that everything in human life has a definite psychological significance, then we have to answer yes to that question.

'When you observe a sleepwalker, you get the impression that the person is *looking for something*. And thus we've immediately found the correct explanation: they can't stay put, there's something they've lost, something they must find again. Liljan only becomes a sleepwalker *after* starting a relationship with Gran; that should put us on the right track. When she walks in her sleep, it's an expression of her trying to get away from Gran. *She's seeking a way back to her brother.*

'Gran was her *premier amour*. Sure, she had been with a couple of men before, but those had just been quick flings; this was her first serious erotic experience. She had "betrayed" her brother for the first time. But her fixation on Werner is constantly the strongest force in her; she actually suffers from a strong feeling of guilt because she's given herself to another man. The two dreams make this clear: she was only able to receive these telepathic impulses at all because she feels impure; she accepts her brother's judgment of her. She loves Werner and unconsciously wishes to be *punished* by him; her love, in other words, is decidedly masochistic. When he demands that she throw herself in the lake, she's forced to obey.

'Needless to say she doesn't react like this when she's awake; if she did she would be insane. But when we're asleep, we're all psychopaths to a certain degree. We no longer have conscious control over ourselves; the subconscious rises up from the depths and runs the mind for eight hours. That's why it's only when *asleep* – when the telepathic connection is strongest – that she becomes a helpless medium. It's during sleep, when all the waking inhibitions and critical faculties are reduced to a minimum, that the pull from her brother draws her to him. And it's when *asleep* that she goes out to return to him for good – that is, to follow his will and drown herself in the lake.

'Gran told us that she had also walked in her sleep the night before we traveled here. She had made her way to the bathroom and had lain down in the tub, which was filled with water. He mentioned it to illustrate how harmless and insignificant this sleepwalking of hers was. But the episode is in no way either harmless or insignificant; on the contrary, it's a very serious *warning*. It reveals a tendency that is starting to surface in her. It's a sort of dress rehearsal, so to speak – the full bathtub is a symbol for the lake!

'Werner quickly finds out that Liljan has been saved, and by the next night he's already coming to the cabin with the goal of taking her life – he wants to take advantage of the thunderstorm to enter the cabin unnoticed. He sneaks along the walls and peeks in through the windows to find her room. He spots women's clothes in one room, assumes they are hers, and clambers in through the open window. He stands there in the darkness, waiting for her – and possibly Gran – to come. He has gone into the wrong room, however – the clothes he saw were Sonja's – and when Bernhard comes in a while later, Werner understands he's made a mistake. Or maybe he gets scared. In any case, he makes a run for it; he seizes the chance to jump out the window again while Bernhard beats a hasty retreat in the opposite direction. Only his footprints reveal that the ghost has paid us a visit.

'A while later, Gran suddenly decides to take up the pursuit; he wants to seize the chance while the prints are still fresh. Armed with a blackjack and a pocket flashlight, he goes out alone into the darkness and follows the tracks through the forest to the lake. Werner is still out there – he has probably remained in the lake's immediate vicinity all this time. He realizes someone is after him and discovers to his satisfaction that it's Gran. In short, he's got an excellent opportunity to eliminate one of his two victims. He creeps up on him unnoticed from behind and gives him a powerful shove into the lake. Gran can't swim, and in his panic he gets completely tangled in the reeds, his legs get stuck in the muddy bottom – he's fallen in at a shallow spot – and he drowns.'

'Now you have to explain how you immediately knew where to find his body,' I said.

'As I said, Liljan told me. That night she dreams she sees Gran's body lying right where he did in fact drown. Yet another proof of the telepathic connection between her and her brother. At this point, it's reached maximum intensity; it's so strong that the ideas and experiences of one of them play out as clear images in the dreams of the other.

'Thus I've acquired a very unusual weapon against Werner. I can constantly keep up with what he's doing; I can get a fix on his plans and objectives – simply by knowing Liljan's dreams! Most detectives wander around with a camera when they're investigating a murder case, snapping photos left and right, hoping to get a couple of nice close-up shots of the murderer in person. But in this case *I* have images of far greater value – I'm following a photographic report of the murderer's own mind!

'That is crucially important to the drama's solution. The same night Liljan also has another dream: she sees herself plunging into Blue Lake, and immediately after the water has swallowed her up, she sees her brother come after her – he jumps out from a ledge and follows her into the depths. And she has a clear sense that this wasn't happening while she dreamt it, but *that it would happen the following night!* The following night, meanwhile, is Gruvik's night, the night of August 22!

'The significance is fairly clear. Werner has sent his sister a final message: the next night she will throw herself into the lake, and he will follow her. However, during her analysis sessions with me, Liljan has gradually become immune to her brother's hypnotic influence. Above all, there's been an important change in the course of the past twenty-four hours, during which time I've exerted all my efforts to save her. The true connection, the secret of her subconscious, has been brought out into the daylight. The neurotic fixation is broken, she has begun to be *cured* of her brother complex. You mustn't think this cure has come about as the result of a few hours of coaxing. There are months of work behind it; the whole time I've been in a violent tug-of-war with that other strange power controlling her. Even as late as the day before yesterday *he* still had the upper hand, but finally the scales tipped in my favor. It's characteristic that her final dream is totally free of symbols and repressed feelings. This time she receives directly, without any ambiguity, what her brother has to say to her.

'There was one other thing that revealed Werner's ultimate purpose. He left behind a document, a bookmark, which typically enough was inside Dante's *Divina Commedia.*'

Bugge pulled out the little paper he had shown me the previous evening. He unfolded it and laid it out in front of us on the table.

'Look at this. It looks like the sort of thing a distracted person scribbles while his conscious mind is busy with some problem. At the top of the page there are three small crosses, and under these crosses are drawn, respectively, a spruce tree, a lily, and the initials B.W. Underneath there are two numbers written: 23831 and 23841.

'He jotted these figures down while distracted, sure enough, but that doesn't make them meaningless. It's his "other person" who wrote them down; in his absent-minded state, he was a medium for his own subconscious. *He wrote down his secret, psychopathic plan.* In this drawing he "announces" three deaths, symbolized quite simply with three crosses, like an ordinary death announcement. Under the first cross there's a spruce tree, the symbol from the dream, Harald Gran; under the second there's a lily, also a symbol from the same dream, his sister Liljan; and under the third cross we find the letters B.W., the initials of his own name, Bjørn Werner. These are the three who must die for the reenactment to be fulfilled. The figures 23831 and 23841 represent the two dates 23-8-31 and 23-8-41. On the 23rd of August, 1831, Tore Gruvik drowned himself in the lake after committing his double murder. On the 23rd of August, 1941, Bjørn Werner would do the same after having committed the corresponding murders. Insofar as Werner became the "reincarnation" of Gruvik, he had to kill himself on the same date!

'There is one other thing that demonstrates how tremendously strong this identification with Gruvik is. And how subtly logical a mentally ill person can be. Tore Gruvik left behind a diary, in which an almost illegible confession showed that he was the murderer. Bjørn Werner leaves behind a diary too, and *in reality that diary contains his confession.* But it is "almost illegible", it can only be read by someone who understands the language of its symbols.

'Now how should I approach the case? Obviously we could have done a manhunt through the woods and sooner or later we would have caught him, but the result would have been that he would have had to spend the rest of his life locked up in an asylum. The most humane thing to do was to let the story play out.

'So I form a simple plan. I know that Werner is going to kill himself the following night; that's apparent both from the document with the "death announcements" and from Liljan's latest dream. But the prerequisite is that he must first repeat Gruvik's deed: the double murder. One of the victims has already been eliminated – all that's left is to kill Liljan. If Werner can be made to believe that he's dragged Liljan with him into death, then he'll immediately make short work of things and drown himself.

'How to make that happen?

'Sonja has a strong resemblance to Liljan; therefore I convince her – in her capacity as an actress – to take on a difficult part, namely the role of murder victim. Sonja is a very good swimmer, which really comes in handy on this occasion. What she'll have to do is the following: at the exact same time when Liljan walked to the lake in her sleep two nights earlier, she will – dressed in Liljan's nightgown – copy her somnambulistic ramble. She'll go out in the dark with her arms stretched in front of her; she'll approach the lake with slow steps and throw herself in, then swim underwater for twenty yards towards a point where the shore is hidden by tall reeds. There, as discreetly as possible, she'll crawl onto land. There's a ninety-nine percent probability Werner will be watching the lake tonight to make sure his sister comes. Of course there's a possibility he'll see through our scheme, in which case he'll make an attempt to break into the cabin and kill her there. That's why I had Bråten stay behind to keep watch in the living room.

'Everything goes according to plan, however. A little while after Sonja disappears below the surface, Werner emerges from the woods, walks to the shore, and stops on the ledge. Suddenly his body is seized in an epileptic fit – a typical symptom in criminal psychopaths – he falls over, and with a piercing shriek – Tore Gruvik's death cry! – he plunges into the lake.

'Bjørn Werner dies with the idea that he's finally being united with his beloved . . .'

★

Bugge had been talking uninterrupted for almost forty-five minutes. The fire in the hearth had gone out. We sat quiet for a long time in the semi-darkness, looking at one another. It was hard to think of anything to say.

'That was a fantastic story,' I muttered at last.

'Agreed,' Bråten chimed in. 'Fantastic to say the least. I've never come across anything like it before.'

Bugge gave a friendly nod.

'I can certainly believe that,' he said.

CHAPTER FIFTEEN

Which isn't a chapter, only a short postscript

THE WEATHER WAS LOVELY when we took the train back the next day. The August sky hung like a cool, crystal canopy over the lush landscape; I stood with my head out the carriage window and drank in long draughts of the champagne-fresh autumn air. We had finally left those woods. I had the feeling of being freed from a powerful spell; it was as though I had just escaped safely from Dante's Inferno.

The wheels droned underneath me. It sounded to me as if they had taken on a new, liberating rhythm – the rolling steel *sang*; it was the dynamic music of the machine, the melody of the twentieth century. Thank God, I was on my way back home to civilization. I would never let myself be lured out into the wilderness again. What was it that loony old Romantic said about going back to nature? Be my guest. He had never set foot outside Paris. And quite rightly too.

Mørk, Bugge, and I had found spots in the same compartment. The two of them were still discussing the events of the past twenty-four hours. I wasn't really following their conversation; I could only tell they were in deep disagreement. As usual. They wouldn't be themselves anymore if they were able to agree on even a single detail, no matter how small or insignificant.

'Others will fault your theory for being far-fetched,' said Mørk. 'But I, on the other hand, fault it for a lack of imagination. You could just as well have given your lecture on telepathy to a meeting of telegraph operators and teenage radio enthusiasts. They would have understood all of it, God help me. Your philosophy is *earthbound*; therefore it's no philosophy at all. It is written: "Do not lay up for yourselves treasures on earth, where moth and rust destroy." Which translates to: don't waste your time with psychoanalysis and other ephemeral truths. Seek the spiritual sources...'

'Thanks, I've already got Doré's illustrated Bible and five bound volumes of *The Scourge*,' said Bugge. 'And that's enough for the time being.'

While I stood at the window deep in concentration, it suddenly struck me that there was still one unresolved problem in this story. I'm not the kind of man who likes to leave a question unanswered; I'm something of a researcher by nature. So I turned to Bugge.

'There is one thing that maybe you wouldn't mind explaining to me,' I said. 'One point that's still a little murky.'

'Which is?'

My friend smiled up at me benevolently. Sort of like a kindly old schoolteacher dealing with his slowest pupil.

'Why did Liljan behave so strangely when she was alone with you in her room? And why did she scream that *you wanted to drown her?*'

His smile vanished. He set his mouth tightly.

'Damn it!' he exclaimed. 'Anyone would think you were part of an international spy ring. How on earth could you have heard...?'

'Oh, it's just some little telepathic abilities I have. But I'm very interested in knowing the connection.'

He was silent for a couple of seconds. It seemed like he was debating whether he should answer the question or just give me a moral lecture. But then he leaned back and crossed his legs.

'All right. Now that you've thrown out that intricate question, I'll have to answer it. Otherwise I'm sure you'll go around gossiping about it and embellishing it with your own clever commentary, and I don't want my good name and reputation being ruined . . .

'So, then, the point of analysis, in simple terms, is the following. The patient is erotically fixated – without knowing it – on a person in their immediate family: mother, father, sister, or brother. In other words, a substantial portion of their life's energy is wasted. It's fixated on an unattainable object, a person they can't possess, and that has a crippling effect on them, makes them unable to cope with everyday life. They're tied to something fictitious, something that drains their strength without giving them any release. They become a prisoner in a cage whose bars they can't even see. The psychoanalyst's task is to liberate this pent-up energy by, so to speak, directing it toward himself. He takes over the role of the unattainable one the patient loves; he will actually *become* the mother, father, sister, or brother. That's what we call *transference* in our scientific jargon.

'And here you have the explanation for the scene you witnessed: during that hysterical fit, Liljan sees her brother in me. Her subconscious speaks through her, she shouts desperately that I want to drown her; in short, she suddenly identifies me with Werner. She attributes *his* actions to me, *his* wish to drown her in the lake!

'That moment represents the crisis point of the analysis, but from then on it's me and not Werner who has power over her. From that point on *I've* taken over Werner's role – *the transference is complete*. That she makes such a violent revolt against the analyst's mental power over her is in itself a good sign. And that she expresses it by attributing her brother's power to me clearly shows that I've won the battle. I've transferred to myself the love that bound her to a phantom. From now on it's me she is bound to, and the only thing left is to remove that fixation once more, release her from the analyst, set her free . . .'

Bugge delivered his lecture fluently and effortlessly, as if reading from a carefully prepared manuscript. I was impressed. But from over in the corner where Mørk was sitting there came some little gurgling noises, like the sound of pebbles being dropped down a well.

'What are you laughing at?' I asked.

'I'm thinking about the article I'm going to write when I get home,' he said. 'I already have the title: "Psychoanalysis, the Great Parody". My fingers are itching to write it. Good God, what an article it's going to be!'

A few more pebbles fell.

'You've just given me an idea,' I exclaimed. 'I have an unborn novel waiting for me at home. Now I've finally got some real material. My fingers are itching too.'

Mørk gave me a friendly look.

'You know I abhor fiction writing,' he said. 'Writing fiction is something people do so they can have an excuse for avoiding honest work. That's why we have three million writers in this country. The talented authors are the worst; they should be drowned in their own ink. The more talent a person has, the more shameless and incorrigible he is. But you are truly talentless, Bernhard, so I believe you have a mission after all. Write your new novel – it will make my article totally superfluous. If you write another one of your books about psychoanalysis, you'll deal it its death blow. For good. It will never recover . . .'

I cleared my throat. 'I think you're both being rather mean to me,' I said. 'I'm afraid I'll have to take reprisals. I'm going to portray you in my book, gentlemen. Do you hear that, Mørk? I'm going to portray you.'

'Doesn't matter,' said Mørk. 'I won't read your book. However, I will *review* it. So I'll have the last word in any case.'

The train rattled its way further on towards Oslo.

NOTES

2   *reproduction at Japanese tempo*: In 1941, fertility rates in Norway were at historic lows, with an average of only 1.83 children born to each woman, while in Japan the figure was almost three times higher at 4.36. Bjerke's observation, then, is a laconic reference to demographic statistics and not a racial slur.

    'as the desert drinks summer rain': A line from the Welsh author Eric Linklater's novel *Juan in China* (1937).

    Paul's excellent precept about women keeping quiet in company: An allusion to the apostle Paul, who wasn't a fan of women talking: 'Let your women keep silence in the churches: for it is not permitted unto them to speak' (1 Corinthians 14:34); 'But I suffer not a woman to teach, nor to usurp authority over the man, but to be in silence' (1 Timothy 2:12).

3   *the Gårholm case*: An allusion to Bjerke's novel *Nattmennesket* [*The Night Person*], which appeared in 1941, one year before *The Lake of the Dead*, and introduced the characters of Kai Bugge, Bernhard, and Sonja. See the introduction for a fuller description of the book.

4   Das Verbrechen als Erlösung: *Crime as Redemption* (German). In *Nattmennesket*, Bjerke's earlier novel featuring Bugge, we're told that Bugge's book was seized and burned as pornographic.

5   *Gyldendal's series of modern novels, volumes 1 to 52*: The Norwegian publisher Gyldendal's series of modern novels ran to 101 volumes in all, published from 1929 to 1959; they were also known as the 'Yellow Series' for the uniform yellow covers. Of the first fifty-two entries, eighteen were American, by authors such as Ernest Hemingway and James M. Cain; Bjerke no doubt has the female characters of such books in mind here.

    'Anyone who looks at a woman': Matthew 5:28: 'But I tell you that anyone who looks at a woman lustfully has already committed adultery with her in his heart.'

6   *Aulestad*: The home of Bjørnstjerne Bjørnson, a Norwegian writer and 1903 Nobel Prize winner; the site is a museum today.

Kristiania Bohemians: The Kristiania Bohemians (Kristiania is the former name of the Norwegian capital Oslo) were a group of artists and writers from the 1880s, the leader of whom, Hans Jæger, was prosecuted and imprisoned for indecency and blasphemy for his book *From the Christiania Bohemians* (1885), which advocated sexual freedom. The comment is obviously ironic, since Borge is a middling writer of potboilers, not an avant garde author.

7   *Des Lebens ungemischte Freude ward keinem Irdischen zuteil*: 'The unmixed joys of life are bestowed on no man.' (German). A line from a 1798 ballad by Friedrich Schiller, 'Der Ring des Polykrates'.

      the Widow of Zarephath's jug: A reference to 1 Kings 17, in which a widow gives food to the Prophet Elijah; God ensures that the contents of her jug never run out.

9   *empty as the fleshpots of our time*: Exodus 16:3 tells of how the Israelites ate well in Egypt, dining on pots of meat ('fleshpots'); Bernhard's comment here may be a reference to meat shortages and rationing during World War II.

10   *Stein Riverton*: Pseudonym of Sven Elvestad (1884-1934), one of the most widely read Norwegian authors of the early 20th century. He was a prolific writer of detective stories; the varying quality of his work is ascribed to the fact that it was mass-produced and often actually penned by other writers.

12   *Sverre Vegenor's landmark work, 'The Yellow Phantom'*: Sverre Vegenor was a pseudonym of Sverre Nicolaisen (1886-1950), who contributed the feature story to 182 issues of *Detektiv-Magasinet*, the first of which, 'Det gule gjenferd' ('The Yellow Phantom'), was published in issue 14 in 1929.

14   *Hamsun's vagabonds*: The Norwegian Nobel Prize winner Knut Hamsun often featured itinerant characters, most famously in *Hunger* (1890), in which a writer wanders deliriously around Oslo while literally starving to death, and *Mysteries* (1892), in which a stranger's arrival in a small town brings unexpected consequences. Bjerke may have a specific book in mind, though, Hamsun's later novel *Landstrykere* (1927) (translated variously as *Wayfarers* or *Vagabonds*), in which two young men wander around Norway seeking wealth, love, and adventure.

15   *Wildenvey*: Herman Wildenvey (1885-1959) was one of the most prominent 20th-century Norwegian poets. In 1940, Wildenvey reviewed the young Bjerke's first collection of poetry, writing, 'It's

a miracle that a young boy can write such elegant verse, whose content and tone at times demand a full command of the language. This is an extraordinarily promising debut . . .' A search of six volumes of Wildenvey's collected poems did not turn up the line quoted by Bjerke.

16 *he who loves his sister should discipline her promptly*: A paraphrase of Proverbs 13:24 ('He who spares his rod hates his son, but he who loves him disciplines him promptly.')

18 *Lill Herlofson Bauer*: Lill Herlofson Bauer (1913-1972) was a Norwegian journalist and author known for her popular novels about young, modern women. With a style that mixed humor and romance, Bauer often wrote about women who rejected traditional gender roles, seeking careers instead of wanting to raise children.

25 *the new bread*: During World War II, rationing and shortages meant that wheat flour was often unavailable; bread began to be made out of alternative ingredients such as soy, whose healthfulness some, like Bernhard here, apparently questioned.

50 *'fragment of a magical life'*: I can find no reference to this phrase except as the title of a collection of poetry by the Norwegian writer Claes Gill, published in 1939. Gill was a Modernist with a reputation as an aesthete; the allusion here is a curious one, since Bjerke was one of the outspoken critics of Modernist poetry.

52 *But before me stood Beatrice, the pure one*: Purgatorio XXXI, lines 79-84. Surprisingly, the first partial translation of Dante's *Comedy* into Norwegian doesn't seem to have appeared until the 1960s. Bjerke has lifted these lines from the mid-19th-century Danish translation by Christian K. F. Molbech, with the spelling lightly altered to conform to Norwegian norms. With apologies to Dante, my translation is of Bjerke's text, not the Italian original.

59 *Maya's veil*: A reference to a Hindu belief that we see life through distorting veils that prevent us from perceiving actual reality. Bjerke might have come across reference to it in the German philosopher Schopenhauer's writings.

81 *Sigurd Hoel*: Sigurd Hoel (1890-1960) was a novelist and short story writer, as well as the editor of Gyldendal's series of translated modern novels, which introduced Hemingway, Fitzgerald, Faulkner, Kafka, and dozens of other key 20th-century writers to Norwegian audiences. Thus, Hoel would be a double target of Mørk's wrath, as not only an author of modern fiction, but also a

translator and publisher of other authors' works. In an obituary, Bjerke wrote that if Hoel had written in English, he 'would have had a worldwide reputation'.

81   *Aksel Sandemose*: Aksel Sandemose (1899-1965) was a Danish-Norwegian writer and one of six finalists for the 1963 Nobel Prize in Literature. His novel *Varulven* (1958; English trans. *The Werewolf*, 1966), which deals in part with the psychology of those who collaborated with the Nazis, occasionally appears on lists of the 20th century's best novels.

103   *Olga Barcowa, the green-eyed adventuress*: One of the detective Knut Gribb's chief adversaries in the Norwegian pulp *Detektiv-Magasinet*, an international adventuress and master criminal whose dark eyes have a hypnotic power.

109   *Kittelsen's paintings*: Theodor Kittelsen (1857-1914) was a Norwegian painter famous for his illustrations of eerie Nordic folklore.

135   *men like Ludwig Dahl, for example*: Ludwig Dahl was a Norwegian judge and mayor of Bergen in the early 20th century. A devotee of spiritualism, he dabbled in the occult and seances, but after his two sons died, his interest grew into an obsession. During a seance in 1933, the medium claimed to have a message from Dahl's son, saying that Ludwig would suffer a fatal accident in August of the following year. On August 8, 1934 Dahl drowned during a visit to the seaside. However, the fact that he had a large life insurance policy set to expire the very next day cast doubts on the role of the supernatural in his death. His daughter and the medium were charged in a plot to kill him for the insurance money; the trial was an international sensation, pitting science against spiritualism. In the end, the jury acquitted them and the death was ruled accidental.

CPSIA information can be obtained
at www.ICGtesting.com
Printed in the USA
BVHW041733130922
646908BV00003B/21